Arizona Blueberry Studios Presents

Jinshiriu

Never Forget Nagasaki

2005

by **Ross Anthony**

Foreword

This is a difficult work to set free into the world. It was, at times, heart-wrenching to write. I feel what my characters feel. I laugh with them, root for them, cry for them. Writing **Jinshirou**, I cried at the keyboard on many occasions.

A harder-edged book than most of my other works, I like to think of **Jinshirou** as an uplifting tragedy. A poem in darks and lights that examines the concepts of honor, hate, prejudice, tolerance, revenge, war, compassion from the inside out. Some people can dig down deep into the dark chambers of their souls and find the power to break the chain of hate. It's like breaking an addiction. Unfortunately, for others, an undoable mistake may be the only thing to prompt that lesson. Hopefully this book will inspire thought in the direction of lessening the number of those mistakes.

Perhaps important to note, I had sketched out the outline of this story prior to the events of 9/11/01. And yes, it is fiction. The characters are not based on any real persons living or dead.

Ross Anthony

Dedicated to Yngve

For other Books, Essays & Articles by Ross Anthony
www.RossAnthony.com/books

Special Thanks
Fae, Eiko, Setsuko, Nobuko, Philip & Fay

ISBN: 0-9727894-3-X ISBN13: 9780972789431
First Printing 7/2005
10 9 8 7 6 5 4 3 2 1   500 7/05

Jinshirou

Never Forget Nagasaki

Like the twilight, he lies in the balance between night and day.

Jinshirou's head rests uneasily against the dimly lit airplane's only unblinded window. He's watching the red ball sunrise hobble out over the soft blue curve of the Earth. His unsettled eyes are fixed, but he is more distant than the horizon. Waking in the balance between night and day, boy and man, homeland and abroad; an ocean froths below. Massive choices, like tectonic plates, vie for position underground.

A red ball bobbing on a sea of white waves, the Japanese flag unfurls proudly on the airplane's foldout video screen. **The edges of the circle weaken. The red begins to bleed across the innocent cloth, soaking the banner in damp fertile blood.**

In the seats next to him, Mother lays peacefully asleep in the arms of Father. Japanese, Americans, citizens of the world, curl in uncomfortable seats, in blankets, in sleep, in dream. Though the jet approaches 750mph, nothing moves but the warping sun, the ocean beneath.

A single plane, a 1940's B-29 bomber, "BOXCAR" painted on its side, passes Jin's aimless gaze. The event is surreal to the contemplative Jinshirou. The Airforce pilot turns his head toward the passenger plane, his eyes encounter Jin's. Frozen, as if by electricity, four retinas burn. Horror overtakes the pilot's face, he turns his head away in shame, soars off sharply.

A gracefully aged woman walks with her quiet grandson, Aro. She gently strokes the long white hair from her darkened wrinkled skin and hooks it behind her ear. Aro holds her other hand. He studies the wreckage of a hardware store. The concrete blocks broken in their own powder. A peaceful breeze tosses a US war propaganda pamphlet. It floats to the ground in front of Aro. He's seen them littering the cobblestone streets many times before: A tall, angry, white-bearded, cartoon man wearing a red, white and blue tuxedo, matching top hat, both arms raised high as he throws warheads from the sky down onto Japan. A word balloon inflates from the cartoon. **"Surrender or the big bomb will fall."**

On this day, the sky is gray, but still clear. An eerie white light illuminates the neighborhood. Aro's grandmother smiles to meet her friend. "Looks like a nice day today."

Her friend smiles back. "I think the sun just might hold back the clouds."

Aro's eyes are fixed on the pamphlet, even at five years of age, he is old enough to understand. A single airplane in the sky steals his attention. The plane sails far off, but Aro can still see something fall from it. Something heavy. Something pointed, like a dagger. The plane darts off at a sharp angle away.

Grandmother's conversation fades, she turns her brown-black eyes, tanned yellow skin to the falling dagger. One by one, friends, neighbors, all join the small boy in his frozen stance toward the city center.

The burst of light reflects across their faces like a camera's flash. Or lightning. They blink, but do not move. A mushroom of dust, dirt, debris begins to grow above the valley. Still the onlookers do not move. Dumbfounded.

Finally, a loud crashing thunder spurs gasps, tears. Some collapse in shock. The boy is spellbound, mouth gaping, eyes wide, eardrums ringing, head tilted in incomprehension. A sudden wind rushes through the little boy's hair, blows the pamphlets up from the street like a flutter of pigeons. Grandmother comes to her senses, lifts the boy to her bosom and begins to run home in a muted panic. A sick saffron hue infiltrates the previous white of day.

The leather-bound diary rests open on a pedestal. Though encased in glass, the hand-written pages seem vulnerable. Ink blue, penmanship precise, hand-pressure light. Two finger-indented buttons are mounted upon the pedestal, one labeled 'English' the other 'Japanese.' A white woman blinks her red-rimmed eyes after viewing poster-sized pictures of charred, dismembered citizens of Nagasaki. The museum, silent despite the stream of visitors. The woman lowers her red-gloved hands from her face, extends a suede-wrapped finger, presses "English." The translated words of Aro's mother vibrate from the installation's eight-centimeter speaker:

It's the tenth day now. My skin is like the shell of south coast shrimp. I can no longer get up to use the toilet. I am sleeping long hours and I do not think I will be able to keep track of these days much longer. My left eye still will not open. Mother brings little Aro to visit me in the afternoons when I am awake. But today, I could not hear him crying anymore. My little Aro, he is the only one now, the only one to carry on our name. My little Aro, what will become of him?

Aro scratches his grizzly white beard. He gently strokes a string of long gray hair behind his ear. Alongside him walks his star pupil, Jinshirou. Robes trailing, they stroll comfortably through the bamboo garden. The temple grounds teem with students of all levels and ages practicing Kyudo, Karate, Aikido, Judo, Sumo, Kendo, swords.

Aro breathes the cool, moist island air. "Jinshirou, you have exceeded my expectations. You have defeated every other student more than once. There are no longer any that possess skill even enough to help you improve yours. In all my years, I have neither taught nor seen others teach such an able student." Aro lifts his stringy white eyebrows. "Beginning tomorrow you and I shall spar. But tonight, you must catch the dove and meet me in the temple's chamber."

At the age of nineteen, Shoji, like Jinshirou, is among the older boys. He turns away from his sparring partner to look as Aro and Jinshirou pass near the temple chamber. Temporarily unguarded, Shoji's face catches the curved arch of his sparring partner's bare foot. Despite the blow, Shoji continues his sober gaze toward his childhood friend and Master Aro. Shoji's practice partner stops too, turning a heavy head in the direction of Shoji's stare. Shoji takes the opportunity to return the face-spanking kick.

Jinshirou runs his callused fingers along the rich wood grain. "Thank you Master, but no one is allowed in the chamber."

Aro grins, "Am I?"

"Yes, you, but no one else."

"Jinshirou. No one is allowed, but those who have caught the dove with their bare hands."

Aro and Jinshirou return to their stroll. Shoji cannot hear their conversation. Like a ballroom decorated with dancers, the temple grounds are all a flutter with sparring. A pair of four-year-olds turn, jab, block. Neither able to get the upper hand, one finally lunges forth in desperation and knocks the other against a wooden pillar. Pigeons fly from the shingled roof above.

Jinshirou sits alone in the dark, sprinkles seeds on the soft brown dirt of the temple grounds. Pigeons crowd to eat them. Jinshirou lunges open hands into them. They rush off rather indifferently, mock his pride, settle right back down to eat. He tries several times more without avail. Checking his watch, he sighs, looks up to the temple chamber window. A small glow from Aro's candles break a square hole of warm light out of the dark temple walls.

Inside his chamber, Aro sits cross-legged on the floor. Candles burn in a circle around. He listens to the wax sliding down to the floorboards. Meditating. Chanting. Preparing for an important ritual. Two small cats wrestle in a fur-muffled silence. A larger crow-black cat, almost sad in its calm, glares upon the tussling two kittens, casts a similar, seemingly disagreeable glare upon Aro, struts passed the wilting candles. With an agile hop up to the windowsill, its blue-black eyes reflect the light of the stars down to Jinshirou.

Jinshirou huffs in surrender, he tosses the rest of the seeds at the apathetic birds, stomps heavily, legs like oars, through the sea of pigeons straight for the gate.

The local convenience store offers snacks, more seeds, and a public phone.

Back in Jinshirou's home, the phone rings. Mother and Father sit relaxing and laughing in front of the TV set.

Mother answers the ring, "Hello?" She nods and looks over at Father. "Okay. Then we'll see you in the morning." She hangs up the phone, but not her worry.

Father, worn out from a hard day's work, but relaxed, smiles, "Was that Jin?"

"Yes, he says he's working on something with Aro and may end up spending the night at the temple."

"He's really impressing Aro these days. Good for him."

"Yes." Mother smiles away her concern. "Good for him."

Jinshirou drops his head to the phone. An animal's scowl disrupts his pause. He walks back to the temple gates and squints up to the blue-eyed cat perched upon Aro's sill. The cat stares straight back. A black bird dips back and forth between, a violin bow against their line of sight. Black bird scratches the black night, teases black cat pounces, launches in half the blink of a blue eye. At once, both bird and cat evanesce. Jinshirou leaps through the gate in an attempt to find their landing. The darkness denies revelation of either feline or fowl.

Jinshirou in pause. Breaks pause, sits in the center of the flock. Cross-legged like Master, eyes clenched closed. Meditating. He listens hard. Hears beaks to seed, wind through leaves. Hears paws on trees. He opens his eyes, sees the large cat clawing an overhead branch. Leaning his head back and to the left, eyelids slip down, Jinshirou thrusts right hand, right paw, right around, catches a white pigeon right as it takes flight. The rest of the flock fly off in a moth-dust cloud. **The boy Aro stands expressionless. Wind-blown war pamphlets fly off like pigeons.**

Wrinkled tired Aro sits on the floor, candles now flattened into puddles surround. The chamber door opens. Jinshirou steps in, flapping bird in his left hand captures the attention of all three cats. Aro does not take his eyes from a torn and faded photo he holds in both hands. Jinshirou waits patiently at the door, the bird calms.

"She was a beautiful woman, Jinshirou, like your mother. She was always there for me. " Aro gently strokes the tattered edges of the snapshot, now some sixty years old. "My father beat her regularly and the white devils blew her skin off."

Jinshirou drops his head in silence, in respect, in sorrow. He's heard the story many times before, all the boys had. But each time his heart heats just the same. "I know. I'm sorry."

"Come, sit."

Jinshirou quietly finds a pillow within the circle of candles, sits.

Aro peacefully touches knuckle to Jinshirou's hand, offering a perch to the captive flyer. Jinshirou softly releases his grip expecting the bird to fly. The dove keeping a nervous eye on three attentive cats, steps trustingly onto Aro's stubby finger. "My father should have been punished. The whole United States of America should have been punished." Strong, powerful, wise Aro whimpers. Tears begin to well, then flow like candle wax to the floor. "They never knew my mother."

Jinshirou again drops his head in respect. Snap. In a swift and sudden twist of the wrist, Aro breaks the pigeon's neck. Ears of cats hike. A feathery gasp escapes Jinshirou's lungs as the soul of a pigeon.

"As was done by my master for me and his master for him, you and I, Jinshirou, shall feast on this bird." Aro breaks open its corpse, pulling off a pinch of bloodied white meat, he eats. The seeds, the bowing black bird, the cats, the ring of candles, Jinshirou watches dreamily, numbly, as if a remote observer. Aro breaks another pinch of raw pigeon meat, brings it to Jinshirou's virgin lips.

"The dove symbolizes inner peace," Aro speaks through bloodied mouth, "flying all around you, yet elusive, difficult to grasp. You must reach with your soul for it. Your hand alone is not swift enough." He hands over another piece of bloody pigeon meat. "It's like the cracker for the white devil's Jesus. You eat the bread to bring a savior into your guts. But the cracker milled from ground wheat has never known flight, cannot bring inner peace."

Jinshirou gnaws, but cannot taste. The bird is chewy like gum. Aro stands, takes the belt from his robe, ties it around Jinshirou's waist. "I must admit to you Jinshirou, that the dove has never brought me inner peace either. I pray to any God that you shall swallow the nirvana that I could never hold down. I can catch the dove, but only vomit its spirit."

With the sleeve of his robe, Aro wipes some blood from Jinshirou's mouth. "There is anger in me larger than life itself. It has been boiling inside for half a century. Soon, it will crack my neck open and swallow me."

Aro evaporates in self-reflection. His expression is that of a boy watching an airplane. He takes a deep breath of candle-carbon air. "Jinshirou," he places his hand on Jinshirou's shoulder, "you have excelled. You are powerful. You are a graduate. I have nothing left to teach you. I offer to you my school. I ask you to replace me."

Jinshirou bursts into tears. Strong, powerful, confident, naive Jinshirou cannot remember ever crying. His steadfast composure dissolves, "Master! I could never replace you!

What about my family? They want me to stay in the University?"

Aro smiles at the small problems of a big boy, a young man. "Calm. Do not ask me those questions. I have nothing left to teach you."

"But Master?"

"Master? You have caught the dove. You have exceeded expectations. Tomorrow, you call me Aro and my students call you Master." Aro walks to the door of the chamber and opens it. "Go now, and do not return unless to accept my school as your own."

Father buttons up his dress shirt, turns into the living room. Finding Jinshirou sleeping in a corner chair, Father runs his hand across his son's hairline and forehead. "Jinshirou, I've accepted a promotion at the company. It's a great position, but it means we will have to relocate. I've already made arrangements and had you transferred to a university there."

Jinshirou wakes from a shallow sleep. "Where?"

"The United States. Isn't that great?"

Jinshirou rubs his eyes, rubs some dried blood from his lower lip, remembers his manners, "Yes, Father. That's great. Congratulations."

Mother enters unnoticed, leaning head and shoulder against the doorway. She gazes at Jinshirou. It's an invisible extended hand, her gaze is. A beam of good intention, caring, and sadness for the vague inner struggle she senses within her only son.

Jinshirou dives into an Olympic size indoor pool. He laps the breadth of the water twice as fast as any other swimmer. His sharp hands dart up and around, break the wet surface stroke after stroke. He releases energy into the water, gallons displace with each stroke. The simple peace of deafening submersion eclipses his worries while he swims. But eventually, even Jinshirou must come up for air. At one end of a pool crowded with other university students, Jinshirou holds his head just above the water, gripping the edge with his right hand, wiping his face with his left. He bobs there for several seconds without opening eyes.

Shoji swims up next to him, waits for Jin to look. Shoji waits nearly a minute to no acknowledgment. He jabs, "Jin, what's with you?"

Jin's eyes open, but his mouth does not.

Shoji's lips almost tremble with a mix of jealously, envy, anger, loneliness. "Jin, is it true?"

"Is what true?"

"You went to the chamber? Nobody goes to the chamber!"

Jinshirou sighs, shakes his head silently.

"Hey! I'm talking to you!" Shoji's eyes growl, "The great Jinshirou! I could have beaten you. I'm not calling you Master!"

"I don't want you to."

"You went to the fucking chamber! That should have been me! I can beat you. You're not my fucking master!"

"You're good, but you can't beat me, and I don't want you to call me Master."

"You're not unconquerable, Jin!"

Jinshirou turns his head, narrowing his eyes, and for the first time faces Shoji. The two, once very close friends, catch in an entangling glare. A bell chimes, clangs against the porcelain tile. The pool empties except for the two.

"You're no master. That should be me. *You call me Master.*" Shoji reaches out and pushes Jinshirou's head underwater. The fray submerges. A wave-net of light knots the two swimmers. Jin slips away, quickly climbs out of the pool uninterested in a fight, heads for the exit. Shoji hops out, grabs a rescue pole, swings its full length toward Jin's back. Jin listens. Hears the air parting with the swing, sees the reflection of light on the tile, remembers the blue-black eyes, the pigeons taking flight. He turns with eyes-closed and hand open. The pole falls into his palm as if its destination, as a train-car coupling. In the flick of a wrist, Shoji's grip is broken, the pole kisses Shoji's temple. Shoji drops easily unconscious and into the water. Jin shakes his head, dives in to rescue. Tossed up on grated concrete like a sea lion, Shoji comes to, coughing.

Jinshirou leans against the wall to rest. "My mother ... My family comes first. I'm going to the United States." He reaches down to poke Shoji in the chest, "Master."

Shoji reprises his cough, catches breaths like fireflies. Jinshirou reprises his step away.

Shoji waits for his pride to resurface. It takes thirty minutes. He dresses, neglects his class schedule, charges back to the temple, finds Aro sitting quietly under a leafless tree in temple grounds. "Master?"

Aro remains motionless. "Yes, Shoji?"

"I have seen Jinshirou"

Still without turning to face Shoji, Aro smiles, "Looks like you saw the back side of his hand."

"He's going to the United States!"

Aro's smile swims off his face, walks away without another word.

Shoji stands impotent.

Up in his chamber, Aro stands in the center of the room. The blue-eyed cat stares at him from a high shelf. Aro stares back. The sun rounds from the south to the west and then sets, twilight flares and fades. The two do not break stares. The pair of kittens again begin to spar, knocking a paintbrush from a table. Aro turns his head to the fallen brush, then back, but the cat is gone. Frustrated, he slides the table aside, opens a cabinet, pulls out a wooden chest. From the wooden chest, he pulls a photo of his mother. But this is one taken after the bomb. This one she is charred. This one she is dying. From the chest, he pulls a very old US propaganda pamphlet. He strikes a match and watches Uncle Sam and the American flag slowly burn.

Two American soldiers sit near the front gate of their Otsu Base. Their feet up on a small table, they play cards and joke. Aro appears behind the steel bar gate.

A soldier rolls his head over toward Aro. "Who you wanna see old man?"

"You." Aro responds.

The soldier smiles at his pal, then stands, squinting now at Aro, "Do I know you?"

The soldier walks over to the gate and leans against it. Aro grabs the soldier's head through the bars. He twists. The soldier struggles but is pinned against the inside of the gate.

Aro answers the soldiers question, "You know my mother."

The second soldier leaps to his feet, fumbles his weapon, nervously directs it toward the two. "Shit! Rick!"

Pillars of reddish-orange sticks line Aro's torso, Rick catches a glimpse of them, but still cannot break free of Aro's seventy-year grip. "He's got a fucking bomb!"

A wire runs up to Aro's headband. Rick sees it through the sweat. "Don't shoot, dude! His head is rigged!"

Aro reaches through the bars, takes the keys from Rick's belt, unlocks the gate, nods to the second soldier. "Hey, Joe, you get help. I want big brass here now."

Soldier holsters gun, rushes off.

Shoji picks through the crowded Kyoto University hallway to Jinshirou. "Did you see Master this morning?"

Jinshirou walks straight passed Shoji. "No. I was in class, like you."

"He was crazy. He had blood on his face. He said he ate ten pigeons."

Jin stops, turns back. "Ten Pigeons?"

"I saw the feathers in his chamber."

"You skipped class *and* you were in the chamber?"

"Uh, I climbed the wall, looked through the window. I wasn't in there. I could see the feathers from the window. And burnt up pictures, an old woman and a flag, American, I think."

"You could see all that from the window? You have excellent sight."

Broiling in embarrassment, Shoji shouts, "Shut up! Aro misses morning workouts and you in the damn chamber! What the hell is going on?"

Jinshirou turns the side of his face to Shoji. Shoji follows him into the student lounge. Their silent conversation is interrupted by a TV newscast. In the corner of the lounge, an empty soda can above, a skateboard and backpack below, Aro on channel 14 between.

REPORTER: The police are still held at bay by the mad bomber at the Otsu US military base.

LT. SAMAKO: Yes, earlier this morning, apparently the man caught the guards by surprise, carrying explosives strapped to his body. The explosives can be triggered by his headband. The unknown man threatens to fall to the ground if we approach. And it would be too risky to attempt to overtake him. As you know, he has tied one of the guards on the ground near him. For now we must wait him out.

REPORTER: Do we know who he is or what he wants?

SAMAKO: We don't know who he is, however he has been chanting an ancient script.

REPORTER: As if preparing a ritual?

SAMAKO: I don't know. My men are working on that.

Jinshirou clicks off the TV in hopes of saving Aro some face. "We must go there now!"

Fearful of the US military, Shoji seizes the chance to take charge. "You go. Someone should settle the young ones at the temple."

Jinshirou shines a hard eye, "You?"

"Would *you* rather stay back?"

"No!" Jin starts off for the military base, grumbles dubiously, "... Master."

Thirty minutes later, Jinshirou pushes through the crowd of reporters, onlookers, and police to a row of US soldiers guarding the front of Otsu gate.

"Jinshirou!" Aro sees his star pupil through the cracks and spaces between soldiers and gapers.

"Master Aro!" Jinshirou runs toward his venerable teacher, tears distorting his vision bumps into one of the soldiers in the row. The soldier shoves Jinshirou aside.

Jinshirou completing his audience, Aro peacefully rolls an American flag out onto the pavement. A US general winces in distaste. Aro is the center of attention, circled by US military at a distance of about twenty or thirty meters, Rick on the ground next to him, whimpering. Aro kneels on the flag and draws a tanto knife. Jinshirou knows the ritual. He runs again toward the row of soldiers, hoping to break the chain, break the ring of armed men, the ring of explosives, the ringing in Aro's ear.

"Where you going, jap?" A soldier shouts.

Completely distracted by emotion, Jin doesn't hear, doesn't see the butt of the second soldier's gun racing toward his cheekbone. The impact of wood to bone is jarring, produces a flash inside Jinshirou's head, affords him a frozen snapshot glimpse: a leaf fallen, a cloud burnt from the sun, a bulldog tattoo on the soldier's forearm. Jin falls to his knees, the snapshot soldiers **fall into white gravestones. Rows upon rows of graves reaching to infinity. "Where is Aro?" A gleaming silver pistol slides against Jinshirou's forehead. The icy barrel stings his steaming skin. "I killed him."**

Jinshirou's eyes open, he's confused to find himself flat on the ground, no silver pistol. Through the legs of soldiers, Aro smiles to Jinshirou, whispers. "Never forget Nagasaki."

Kneeling, Aro holds blade to belly. A single last thrust, left to right, Aro's eyes ignite with the sight of his own blood spilling out onto the American flag. He begins to fall back, fall forward. Soldiers scurry like pigeons. They fly away from Aro. Forty-five degrees to the pavement, soldiers dive behind trees, cars, trucks, Humvees. Jin closes his eyes. Aro's head strikes the tarmac like a match. Jinshirou, on all fours, cries, a silent scream, "No!"

Aro's carcass confronts the flag and explodes, setting Jin's eardrums ringing. Splattering drops of his master's blood pock Jinshirou's open-mouthed face. Soldiers all safe.

Only Aro is dead, dismembered. Pigeons glide in from the sky. They find pieces of Aro, peck, pick, eat.

Jinshirou's head rests uneasily against the dimly lit airplane's only unblinded window. He's watching the red ball sunrise hobble out over the soft blue curve of the Earth. His unsettled eyes are fixed, but he is more distant than the horizon. Waking in the balance between night and day, boy and man, homeland and abroad; an ocean froths below. Massive choices, like tectonic plates, vie for position underground.

In the seats next to him, mother lays peacefully asleep in the arms of father. Japanese, Americans, citizens of the world, curl in uncomfortable seats, in blankets, in sleep, in dream. Though the jet approaches 750-mph, nothing moves but the warping sun, the ocean beneath, and Jinshirou's family from Japan to America.

A bearded black professor teaches class in an auditorium. The edges of his beard frost into white. Some students page through comic books, others sleep, a few hold their heads up, take notes.

"So to find the velocity in this equation..." The professor scans the room, "...we do what?"

Jinshirou scans the room as well. He seems surprised, even slightly shocked, that no one has an answer to offer, not even a guess. He raises his hand.

The professor's eyebrows hike, he nods toward Jinshirou who responds, "One deribative."

"First derivative. That's right. And then to find the max and mins?"

Again both the professor and Jinshirou look around, wait. Again Jin raises his hand, this time some disgust for the ignorance of American students slips from his manner. "Second-ew deribative."

In his new dorm room, Jinshirou unpacks the last of his things. Sets up a small Buddhist shrine, carefully laying out a bowl of sifted ashes, some fruit and the photo of Aro's charred mother. In the corner he lights incense, chants.

His Japanese-American roommate, David, stumbles in. Surprised to find Jin on his knees, David pauses his step, backpedals, "Whoa, sorry man."

Jin doesn't flinch, makes no notice, not even a hesitation in the chant. David steps respectfully out, quietly closing the door to the room. He brushes backward into his best friend Ollie.

Ollie clips through the hallway. "What's up dude? There a wasp in your room or somethin'?"

David smiles, changes the subject, "A wasp? No... Nothin'. What's up with you?"

"Nothin'." Ollie gives David a friendly head shove as he confidently passes. "Oh, 'Got that electronics test today. I'm gonna kick some logical butt."

"I'd wish you luck, but why waste it on you?"

"That's the attitude!"

Jin completes his rituals, places the photo into a small drawer aside the miniature altar. Rises to his feet, bows several times. Then turns to open the door, leans out into the hall.

David stands at the next doorway hanging with his dorm buddies Carlos and Skinner. He notices Jinshirou looking at him. "Hey, sorry man. I didn't know you were, well... I mean, it's cool. Hope I didn't disturb you."

"Nossing problom," Jin replies, "solry I detained you."

"Detained? Jeez, forget it man. Hey, look, there's the Portland game tonight. Come see me play."

"Game?"

"Football." David jests, "I'm our star receiver."

Carlos shouts out of view, "Retarded receiver!"

David's not ashamed. "Okay, so I'm like the third throw, but occasionally a ball comes my way." Out of Jin's view, he flips Carlos his middle finger, then steps toward Jin repeating the invitation, "So now that we're roommates, you're gonna have to come watch me play."

"Mmm. Okay." Jin nods.

Skinner hops out into the hallway, his hair three days unwashed, donning a 1980's Terminator shirt and boxer shorts. Struggling to open a jar of peanut butter, his socked feet slide across the floor. "Hey Jinshi dude, bring some brewskis -- I'm havin' a tailgater after the game!"

Jinshirou quickly looks away, makes no response. He and David walk into their dorm room.

Carlos comments to Skinner, "Jinshi? Isn't that like raw fish?"

Jinshirou, leans toward David and whispers, "Are all Amerlicans ridiculrous?"

"What? Those guys?" Unable to discern whether Jin is joking or serious, David replies with an all purpose chuckle, "...As a matter of fact, yes!"

"Isn't this wonderful! I can't believe they just lent us their place. They don't even know us." Father unpacks his briefs into a white dresser. The carpet feels so soft under his feet, the bed so huge, the window grand, the yard endless.

Mother makes a mental note of the room's order. "You think Jinshirou is doing okay?"

"He's as strong as an ox. What makes you think he'll have problems?"

"I don't know. His English isn't very good."

"His English is fine."

"It's just that he's never experienced such a traumatic change in his life before. We've always lived in the same house. He might be strong, but he..." Mother's eyelids drop, a remembered image of Aro on the news crosses behind them, " ... he just sometimes takes things very seriously. That's all."

"I know what you mean, sometimes I think he's more mature than we are." Father closes his suitcase. "Wow, this house is so big!"

"SDFU SDFU SDFU!" South Dakota Falls University cheerleaders incite the crowd. The crowd raises banners, volleys beach balls, sways their arms in one large wave. A young man in a bobcat costume jogs onto the field. The cat's smile never changes. Its paws clap in time with the cheerleaders' bounce, the trumpeting band's march.

Skinner and Carlos jump to their feet. "Meow!"

An agitated Jinshirou searches this stadium full of giddy Americans for something less abhorrent. He scans the row of flags waving at the upper rim. The South Dakota State flag, the school flag. The American flag unfurls violently while the others seem limp. The furious waving captures his full attention. His heart heats as the red strips begin to bleed into the white ones. Then, against the blue, against the white stars, Aro's blood splatters. Though many tens of meters away, a globule splashes Jin's eye. In the stands next to Carlos and Skinner, Jinshirou squeezes watery eyes closed.

Not known for insight, Carlos senses Jin as somehow out of the game night spirit. "What's up, dude?"

Jinshirou recalls the present, then responds evasively, "I cannot-ew understand dis game."

"What? Football?" Carlos is confounded. In his entire life, he'd never encountered a male creature uninformed about football.

Skinner jumps in, "Dude, it's like this... run the ball across the end line there and you get six points..."

"Extra point if you blast it through the posts," Carlos continues.

"Brlast?"

Carlos remembers, "Oh, yeah, the special teams guy, like, all he does -- all he does is just kick the ball through those two posts."

Skinner clarifies, "Goal posts."

Carlos and Skinner pass and kick football dogma without pause until a loud siren horn signifies the end of the first half.

ANNOUNCER: And now for tonight's halftime activities... SDFU is proud to welcome the COIT ceremonies. How about a warm welcome for the College Officers in Training!

A marching band leads a military procession of COIT students. The lead COIT student carries a bloodstained US flag onto the field.

ANNOUNCER: Every year the outstanding cadet is given his officer's stripes ahead of graduation as a tribute to his hard work and dedication to this great country. And this year our ace cadet is: *Second Lt.* Arlen J. Williams.

Jinshirou's eyes fix on this lead COIT cadet as he posts and salutes the bloody flag.

ANNOUNCER: And to award the stripes today we have retired Major Thomas Williams, a pilot in WWII and the Korean War.

MAJOR: ... and grandfather of Arlen J.! I haven't been this proud since VJ day in '45.

To Jin, the "V" and "J" sting like the butt of a rifle to the face.

Arlen, in full uniform, steps up to the platform, salutes his grandfather and the white-haired officers, receives his medals, stripes. On the podium in front of him is a dismantled rifle. Part by part, hands as meticulous as a flautist's fingers, Arlen reconstructs the weapon as if from clay.

ARLEN: My rifle. My rifle is my blood brother, my trusted companion, my wife. Without it I am powerless and without me, it is powerless. I trust my rifle more than I trust my own mother. I know my rifle better than I know this world. I will aim and shoot the enemy before he shoots me. I will not miss.

ANNOUNCER: Give it up for AJ Williams!

The letters "A" and "J" drift across the video screen scoreboards. The "A" tips upside down into a "V." AJ completes the firearm that completes him. He begins to spin the weapon like an airplane propeller, like a dragonfly about a staff of sugar cane.

The rifle - a bamboo stick. AJ - Aro. The bamboo now a poolside rescue stick and Aro now Shoji. Then Shoji - AJ, the stick - a rifle, the butt of which whips around and into Jinshirou's cheekbone.

AJ stops the nickel-plated twisting rifle on a dime. The crowd goes wild with pride. Wide-eyed and ready, the roar continues into the second half. Jinshirou also readies himself for another round. The second half is a blur to him.

SDFU in possession, down by five. They've run the ball up field with steady success, but with no more than twenty seconds on the clock and one down left to cover thirty-five yards, coach calls a time out.

"Ah, shit. We're gonna have to drop it in the end zone anyway," Coach scratches his head. "Wykowski or no Wykowski."

Carlos and Skinner shout down field, "SDFU -- FU buddy -- FU!" In between their beer spilling and senseless cheering, they sincerely attempt to teach their new friend the game of football. "So like Jinshi dude, we're down by like five, but don't let that worry you. I mean like a field goal isn't enough points." Skinner makes the shape of the goal posts with his fingers.

"But," Carlos encourages, "like we said a touch down... remember that word *touch down*? That's what we need now."

"And don't worry, cause like twenty seconds is still sufficient." Skinner points out.

Carlos scoffs, "Sufficient?"

"Yeah, I got that one from Jinshi man. I sound almost like a grad student, huh?" Skinner shines in stupid pride.

Carlos chuckles facetiously, "Almost like."

ANNOUNCER: Fourth and three, nineteen seconds left on the clock. Thirty-four yards to go. SD's got no choice; they've got to go for that TD. QB Frank Chiles is back, he'll be looking for the open man.

Play resumes, teams line up, **HIKE!** Frank back steps, fakes, scours the end zone. David is wide open.

Carlos screams, "Oh! Oh! Check it out! Dude! David is wide open! Hit David, dude!!!"

Frank catches a glimpse of David amidst the scattering jerseys. He fires. The spiraling football arches forty-eight yards, directly toward David, but two feet too high. David's two feet leap, but the ball sails out of reach. Game Over. SDFU loses.

Skinner shouts down from the stands, "Oh my god, Chiles, you suck!"

"Suck?"

Carlos turns to Jin, "You know, blow, reek, ... suck!"

As SDFU exits, a player mocks Frank, "Portland pay you to throw like that or did you do it for free?"

Frank, practiced at passing the blame, scans the end zone, finds David. "Ask Yokoyama. I put it right in his hands."

Frank leaves the crowd of SD players to storm David at the tunnel's mouth. David, used to Frank's pettiness, isn't upset by the desperate shove.

"What? Did you lose it in the sun?" Frank shoves David again as the two walk to the locker rooms. "You fucking chink."

David attempts to dilute Frank with humor. "Yeah, it's these slanted eyes. Hard to see out of 'em. No peripheral vision."

Frank continues riding David, "Hope you're happy! You lost the fucking game for us."

David stops at the water table. "Get a grip, Frank. It was high and outside."

Having taken Jinshirou down to the locker room hallway, Carlos and Skinner await David.

Frank's girlfriend, Lucy, and her red-haired friend, Rhonnie, also wait for the team.

"Whoa, babes!" Carlos notices Rhonnie and Lucy.

Skinner nods, confident that he will make no moves, "And they are looking very sufficient."

"Uh oh..." Carlos warns.

"What? What, dude? You okay?"

"He's getting excited..."

"Who?"

"Carlos Jr."

"Oh... that is so sick. I didn't want to know that."

Helmet in hand, but otherwise still in full undirtied uniform, Frank stomps toward Lucy. He chugs ice water from a paper cup.

Lucy sends a sympathetic smile, "Good game, Frank."

"Fuck you, bitch." Frank tosses his cup of water into Lucy's face.

Aro's father slaps Aro's mother. The sound of roughened palm to softened cheek echoes down the hallway.

Jin steps swiftly to Frank. "Aporlogize to dis woman."

Frank's face reflects that of a child refusing to obey somebody else's mother. "Get out of my face, dude. This has nothing to do with you."

Frank grabs Lucy by the hand. " Come on, let's go."

Jin turns to Rhonnie, he points at her soda cup. "May I bahlrow dis?" Rhonnie nods. Jin empties its contents on Frank's head. Frank freezes in surprise.

"I aporlogize," Jin flicks the paper cup into Frank's face. "See how easy? You trlie."

Eyes raging red and wet, Frank lunges at Jin. Shoulder pads strike shoulders. Precise strokes pound in quick progression, finding flesh between pads. Frank cannot remember the contact that transpired between lunge and fall. Jinshirou pins Frank to the floor, "I aporlogize-ew ... *You say it now!*"

Flat on his back and gritting his teeth to hold back embarrassing tears, Frank Chiles softly cries out, "I'm sorry, dude!"

"Not to me, *dude.*"

Frank stops gritting, relaxes between heavy breaths, then sighs. "Lucy, I'm sorry. I ah, I apologize."

Lucy smiles, cries. Rhonnie beams in awe. Jinshirou's gallantry has left a shining impression on her heart, a proof coin on a velvet pillow.

Ever the diplomat, upon finding the two on the ground, David opts for levity. "Hey Frank, watch out for that third down blitz."

David nods to Carlos and Skinner, then pats Jin on the shoulder. "Come on, let's get outta here."

Jin steps off Frank. Carlos and Skinner silently make faces. David puts his smelly arms around the three. "Frank isn't really worth getting sweaty over. Still, it was kinda fun to see him apologize to somebody. For that, my new roomdude, I'm buying the beer tonight."

The two goofs impulsively exclaim, "BEER!"

As the group reaches the parking lot, David pulls keys from pocket, heads for his car. "The beerman cometh -- ooga ooga."

Aro sharply grabs a young Jin by the arm after the boy has been giggling.

Suddenly and seriously Jin grabs David by the arm. "Neber forget-ew Nagasaki."

A suddenly serious David jerks his arm free from Jinshirou's overbearing grip. He stops in his tracks and watches dumbfounded as Jinshirou, Carlos, and Skinner walk off to the tailgate party.

Carlos misses the nuance of that last exchange, speaks. "Cool. I heard about that rice wine stuff you guys drink in Japan."

Skinner turns back at David and shouts, "Yeah, Davie Dude, get two bottles of that Nagasaki shit and don't forget the chips, neither!"

David slowly turns his back to them. His resilient optimism, distant diplomacy, and level demeanor wrestle silently with Jinshirou's sharp blow.

Jinshirou follows his two new friends to the other side of the parking lot. Coeds hang out of vans, trucks, trunks, guzzle six packs, drink till drunk. Jin looks in disgust on this foolhardy lot of Americans, the three come across a group of COIT guys spilling out the back of a huge red pickup. Some in it, some sitting on kegs, Arlen J., center of the clan, ass in a lawn chair as a bulldog tattoo dyes into his forearm. The music pounds, thumps, plastic vibrates. Cigarette smoke, pot smoke, burn his eyes, but Jinshirou cannot stop staring at the tattoo. The needle punctures, Arlen grimaces.

Carlos shakes his head. "Shit, that's gotta hurt."

Skinner shoves Carlos. "Hey, doesn't your sister got a cherry tattoo on her thing?"

"How do you know about that?"

"Everybody knows about that."

A COIT student jerks his chin at Jinshirou's gaping. "Gotta a problem, geek?

Carlos and Skinner grab onto Jinshirou like a couple of rodeo clowns. "Whoa, Bruce Lee, not these guys."

"They're not pretty, but they got guns."

Jin ignores the macho COIT chin, his eyes are fixed on Arlen passing out drunk, tattooing that bulldog to his flesh. Arlen's buddy steps directly in front of Jin, then falls to the ground, a concrete gravestone. One by one, each of the Americans fall to the ground, become gravestones, blades of grass rise between.

"Yo, yo, hello?" Carlos and Skinner work together to reel Jinshirou back on course. "Come on Jet Lee -- keep your eyes on the prize."

"Yeah, BEER!" They pull Jin out of the cracks. But Jin's head is still cocked back, eyes piercing the blades of grass rising in the cracks between gravestones. Carlos whispers to Skinner, "Ah, come on Skinner, I think now would be a great time for one of your stupid jokes -- don't you know any jokes?"

"Just that one. But you know it already."

"I think Jinshi could really use a good joke -- come on you idiot, tell him one."

"Oh, okay, so like there's two guys walkin' down an alley and one of 'em has his um, his wanker, you know his wienie, you know, his thingy hanging into a jar of peanuts. So the other guy says... Hey Jin, you know what the other guy says?"

Jin shakes his head, he takes a deep breath. The gravestones disappear. He looks Skinner right in the eyes. "No skin-dude, I don't know. What does da ozzer guy says?"

"The other guy goes, 'Hey, what are you, fuckin' nuts?"

Carlos jerks hard into a fake laugh, "Hah, that's funny! That is so funny. Don't you think it's funny Jinshi?"

Jin almost smiles, but only out of confusion, "Fuking nutz-ew?"

"Yeah, fucking nuts," Carlos explains, "that's like another word for crazy." Carlos relaxes, "Never mind, it's just a stupid joke."

"Or like if you're really pissed at someone, really mad," Skinner continues, "you could say, 'I'm gonna kick you in the fuckin' nuts, you jerk!" Skinner throws his knee toward Carlos's crotch.

"Woah there, brainless!" Carlos deflects, "you've taken your eyes off the prize!"

"Oh yeah!" Skinner remembers, "that's what we were talkin' about... BEER!"

In some anonymous dorm room, Carlos, Skinner and David wake up to the harsh noon sun.

Skinner rolls over. "I don't feel so good."

"Get the hell off me, dude," Carlos shoves him further. "I got a killer headache."

"Man, what kind of condition would you guys be in if we'd actually won last night's game?" David shakes his head.

Carlos fidgets in his seat, doodling on his notes as the English teacher rambles on, "Let's take an ordinary nursery rhyme and tear it apart structurally, okay? Remember this one?" The professor continues seriously and maturely, "Jack be nimble, Jack be quick, Jack jump over the candlestick."

Carlos whispers to Jinshirou, "And burned his balls."

Jinshirou looks at Carlos, then the professor, then closes his eyes in hope that everything might disappear, slip into the cracks in the tarmac.

The moment class lets out, Jinshirou heads without discussion to the school library. Carlos isn't sure, but suspects that he may have annoyed Jin.

Online, Jinshirou spends the rest of the day reading about COIT rituals, schedules, tattoo traditions. The library's computer monitor reflects off his cornea. "Dis is the firlst day of my Amerlican education."

By evening he logs off, clears the browser's history, and heads back to the dorm. Since David is gone, Jin strips to his shorts, begins his work out.

Across the quad, the girl's dorms lay. Lucy smiles on the phone to Frank. Rhonnie tosses her soapy novel in exchange for a long look out the large dorm windows. Across the quad, Jin's window dimly lit by a single candle. Removing his shirt, the candle lights and shadows his rolling abs and ripped obliques. Rhonnie leans her head against the glass, glad she put her book down.

Lucy finishes with Frank, notices Rhonnie's gawking. "It's that buff oriental guy that spanked Frank's butt, isn't it?"

Rhonnie doesn't respond, instead she silently counts the floors, squinting her eyes, pointing an index finger. Seven floors up, Five windows from center, Jinshirou's room. "I'm goin' to the cafe," Rhonnie grabs her purse. "Want anything?"

Lucy snorts, "Yeah, right."

Jin finishes with the muscles, begins on the soul. On his knees facing the corner, candlelight illuminates the picture of Aro's mother. In the other corner, a dozen roses.

Knock knock.

Jinshirou sighs, stands, bows, snuffs the candles. "Enter."

"Entering..." Rhonnie smiles, "I... I hope I'm not disturbing you." A wisp of smoke from a snuffed candle passes, the roses cause her pause. "I can come back."

Jinshirou offers no response. Rhonnie's feeler unanswered, she's left to make the choice herself. "I'm ah, Rhonnie, Lucy's my roommate."

Jinshirou peers directly into Rhonnie's eyes, deep penetrating connection, and yet, sharply piercing, unsettling, even frightening. The longer she dares not look away, the less she feels challenged. Rhonnie again attempts a kickstart to conversation, "Yeah, you stood up for her. You made her boyfriend apologize. I, ah, I thought that was really cool." Nervous pause, "And I just wanted to say... thank you," less nervously, " personally."

Jinshirou nods his head in acceptance of gratitude.

Just barely comfortable with such direct eye contact, the silence begins to vibrate like the wings of a bee. Too excited to leave, the normally rather assertive Rhonnie nods back uncertain, waits for something else to say.

Jinshirou had seen American women on TV, and the Caucasian tourists at Kyoto center, but he'd never cared to look. He never thought that a white woman could be so beautiful. Practice, work outs, school, duties at home, duties at temple, never a second to think about women at all. Girls are for stupid guys like Skinner and Carlos to waste their time on. Nevertheless, Jin cannot find will to break his gaze. This woman's eyes are deep, un-intimidated by Jin's piercing stare, swallowing it. The skin, like porcelain saki bottles; the hair, autumn on Mount Fuji.

Rhonnie clears her throat, "Hey, so, I'm on my way to the cafe. Do you..." She points at him, "... care to join me?" Points at herself. Notices the special corner, "... I mean, if you're not busy."

"No, good idear. I will shower."

"Uhhh, No? Meaning yes? Yes it's a good idea?"

Jin nods.

Rhonnie breaks a smile that beams a glaring light that almost shakes the mighty Jinshirou. "Sure, I'll meet you down there then," she confirms.

"No, you wait here fibe minutes-ew."

This time, Jin's "no" is much sharper, like a command. It bounces against Rhonnie like a rubber bullet. She turns to leave in spite, but decides she may very well be misinterpreting intention. After all, he did agree to join her. "Oh, okay." A smidgen of sarcasm, a mild verbal mock, intended to reaffirm pride, squeezes out. "Me wait here."

Jinshirou grabs a towel, walks across the hall to the showers. Rhonnie snoops the makeshift shrine, reaches for the little drawer, Aro's mother hides inside it. Her curiosity falls pray to worries, sacrilege, abandons the drawer, turns attention to the roses. Touches the little envelope attached to the flowers. Holds it up to the light, but it is empty, whispers, "Now, who could this be for?"

A puddle under the shower room door directly across the hall, Rhonnie catches a glimpse of Jin's upside-down reflection in the water. She gets closer, checks to make sure no one's near, kneels in the hallway in front of the door.

Across the quad, Lucy moves to the window, squints eyes at Rhonnie on her hands and knees in the boys dorm. Lucy's jaw slowly lowers. "Girl? What are you doing?"

Jin cuts the shower's spray, Ronnie scurries back into his room, calming her shortened breath. She sits on the bed, then feeling somewhat presumptuous, moves to the window pretending to enjoy the view.

Jinshirou shuffles in, buttoning his shirt. "Good idear, the cafe." He smiles, "I owe you soda."

Rhonnie sneers at Lucy looking at her from the girl's dorm. "Yeah," She chuckles nervously, "that's right, I guess you owe me a soda."

"Do you hab a car?"

"More or less..." She turns her back to Lucy, realizes Jin's a bit confused by her words. "Yes. Yes, I have a car."

"Can you drlibe me to da bus-ew station after?"

"Sure... then you know what? Let's just grab some food and take it up to S-mountain. There's a good view from there."

Jin throws a handful of clothes in a bag, grabs a few books, and the flowers. "Mmm. Okay."

Jin digs into his noodles with chopsticks.

Rhonnie slurps her soda. Still finding conversation a much more daunting task than she'd ever expected, she indulges in any thought that crosses her mind. "Wouldn't a hamburger have been a bit easier?"

"No."

"Come on, everybody likes hamburgers."

Jinshirou looks up, again piercing his eyes into hers. He chews.

Tiring of the careful and uncareful conversation, Rhonnie settles back into her assertive self. "I drove you all the way up here. You gotta tell me who the roses are for."

Jinshirou smiles while chewing. He pauses to enjoy Rhonnie's impatience. "My moszer."

"Your mother?"

"Yes, mothzer."

Jin continues eating, looks out into the distance below. Rhonnie stares at him smiling. Again beaming. Again impressed with the gallantry.

Off in the distance, a plane flies away, a silent mushroom cloud rises. Aro whispers, "Never forget Nagasaki."

Jin's eyes water, he shuts them tightly, quickly looking down and away.

Rhonnie empathizes, "Do you miss her?"

"Who?"

"Your mother... in Taiwan, or whatever."

Jinshirou reprises his sharp **"No!"** He pauses. "No... I mean, mean, she is here." He points down into the valley, where the mushroom cloud had been. "Down zere in Sioux Falls-ew. She is why I am here arlso."

Rhonnie doesn't understand. Why did he look so sad for that moment? It doesn't make sense if his mother is here... But he's finally talking, she's happy to listen.

"My fathzer transferred here. Better pay, better title."

"You could've stayed back? Right? I mean you're a junior. Carlos told me that. You got less than two years, if you didn't think you'd like it here, I mean you could have stayed in, um, Asia. Right?"

"You cannot understand-ew familry. Amerlicans don't know familry."

"Are you implying..." Rhonnie feels herself dipping into verbal sparring mode. She stops herself. She can sense there's something deeper here on his end, so she decides to let it go, tactfully changes the subject. "Uh, you repaid the soda, but, I'm afraid I don't even know your name."

"Carlos-ew torld ⎪you my year, but not my name?"

"He told me he was pretty sure he wasn't pronouncing it correctly."

"Jinshirou."

"Jinshirou? That's your name?"

"Solry, I hab no easy Amerlican name, like John or Flrank."

"No, that's okay. That's fine. I just, I just didn't know it. Thank you, Jinshirou." Rhonnie relaxes, finally a conversation, "I'm Rhonnie."

"Lronnie ... thzat's a boy name."

"Yeah, right. No... well, it's short for Veronica."

"I am Japanese. Not Chinese-ew. My moszer is not from Taiwan."

Rhonnie smiles at her error, pauses and changes the topic again. "So, Jinshirou, you dance?"

"Dance?" Jin chuckles.

"Yeah, dance, like to music." She stands up to show off a step or two. "What kind of music do you like?"

"I don't listen much-ew."

"Great. But you've got to dance. They've got to have dance back in your country. Wouldn't you like to see how we do it here?"

"You cannot understand. Dancing is..."

"... Is this so difficult for you? I'm asking you out! You brooding Japanese... gallant man! This Irish American red head is asking you out!"

"Asking me out?"

"You know, like a date. You don't have to think of it as a date if you don't want to... but like a date."

"In Japan, thse woman... she neber do thzat. The man do thzat. A good woman..."

Rhonnie doesn't curb her steam. "Yeah, well, look around! You aren't in Japan! Are you? And in case you're too wrapped up in your goddamn chopsticks, there's a good woman sitting right in front of you. There's a dance tomorrow at the Union, I'm asking you to be my date!"

Jinshirou fears not a single man in Kyoto, but this red-haired woman makes him nervous. He puts his head down in his noodles, in embarrassment, laughs at himself.

Rhonnie chuckles to see Jin so perfectly break his stalwart face.

"I, uh... I visit my parlents on weekends-ew."

"That's right, the flowers, the lift to the bus station. I should've... I'll give you a rain check."

"Lrain check?"

"It's just a phrase. It means the offer still holds. We were rained out this weekend, so you can accept, take me up on it, on a sunnier day. Deal?"

"I understand."

Rhonnie pulls out a pen and scratches something on a napkin. "Rain Check. Good for one dance with the lovely Veronica McKale." She finishes and hands the napkin to Jin.

Jinshirou smiles, "Domo arigato." He remembers his manners, unzips his handbag, pulls out a cheap bamboo flute. "For you."

Rhonnie smiles at the obligatory return gift and shakes her head. "Did anyone ever tell you, you're way too serious?"

A rush of thoughts, words, even feelings waft up to Jinshirou's tongue. He bites them. Chews them. Swallows them. Inside they rage, but outside only a small increase in moisture rims his left eye. He forces a smile, "Must be... culrture shock."

Rhonnie studies the moisture, it doesn't seem an appropriate match with the remark. She too curbs her many thoughts in exchange for a safe thing to say. "Thank you for the flute."

Deciding to act on at least one threatening emotion, Jin pulls a single rose from the dozen and slides it into Rhonnie's red hair.

Eleven long stemmed roses rest in a vase to the left of Jin's mother as she prepares breakfast. Jinshirou leans against the wall watching her. "How long will you be living here?"

Mother looks over to him. "You shouldn't take for granted the generosity of others."

"Where are the people who live here?"

"They're living with some relatives out of town. It's kind of them to lend us the place."

Jinshirou's father parks the rented car in the driveway. Jin leans to look out the window. "How's Dad?"

"He's doing very well. He's been looking forward to this for years. He's very excited."

Jin drops his head, wishes he could share his father's enthusiasm. But he simply cannot. Having hoped the US would win over Jin, a subtle shade of disappointment emanates from Mother's skin.

Father skips in, his cheer contrasts. "Great to see you, Jin. How's school going? I found a couple of nice looking homes today!" Father kisses his wife. "So, son how is school? Any problems catching up?"

Jinshirou chortles, "Catching up? No. No problem." Feeling that his family expects more conversation, Jin offers small talk, "I watched a football game."

Father smiles, "That's great. Did the home team win?"

Jin chuckles again, "No."

The windows break from all sides, a team of COIT boys swings into the borrowed home. Jin fights them off one by one, desperate to save his parents. But there are simply too many foes. Swarming like wasps around a hive. Mother and Father cower in the corner. AJ steps powerfully through the front door. He flashes his tattoo at Jin, laughs, draws his pistol. POP. POP. Kills Mother and Father with two shots.

Jinshirou gasps and sits up in his bed. He realizes he's sweating, realizes it's two in the morning, that his parents are sleeping, hopes his grunt hasn't awakened them.

In the master bedroom Father sleeps. Jin's grunt and heavy breathing keep Mother awake. She opens her eyes, but doesn't get up. Helplessness covers her like a blanket.

"And so with the close of the war in the European theatre, the US could turn its attention to Japan. That fight had been dragging on. Japan making a lot of ground, but also taking a terrible toll in damage on its homeland, barraged by conventional bombs, it just would not surrender." The professor taps Skinner's desk with his pointer.

Skinner looks up confused. "What?"

The professor continues, "Finally, the US decided to drop an experimental weapon on the city of Hiroshima, the atomic bomb. The results were devastating, but Japan still would not surrender. So another bomb was set to be dropped on Saga, but weather conditions over that city were poor, so the bomb was dropped during a clear sky over Nagasaki. The irony is that Nagasaki nearly always has rain."

Adjacent to the history building, the sports complex stands. Five COIT students practice their routines; spinning rifles, salutes, in-step marching. Arlen J., front and center, leading.

Richard, Arlen's right-hand man inspires, "Guys, we've gotta get this thing right! The ceremony is tomorrow at 1200 hours. Come on now, pull it together for Arlen."

Arlen runs them through, finishes one routine. "Halt. At ease. Okay, let's do it again."

From a ceiling platform high above, Jinshirou watches the routine closely, memorizing each footstep Arlen J. makes. Tape marks guide on the gym floor.

"And, all right, halt." Arlen relaxes his neck. "That's it, gentlemen. You're looking good. I think we'll have it down after one more go. Rendezvous tomorrow at 0500 hours for practice before the ceremony."

The group of cadets exits.

Jinshirou studies the available implements: wires, lights, ropes, pulleys. Leaps over a short railing, drops five or six feet to a narrower platform, still high in the ceiling. The next platform some fifteen feet below, he leaps to it.

Jin strikes the pool feet first, descends into underwater peace, rests at the bottom, water beats against his eardrums.

Rhonnie squints her eyes through the pool fence. She's excited to have caught a glimpse of Jin, walks around to surprise him.

David grabs his football helmet from a shelf on the dorm room wall. He glances over to Jin's special corner and pauses. He slides the helmet back on the shelf and squats in front of Jin's alter, considers if he should open the small drawer or not. His eyes narrow like those of Jinshirou's mother. "Who are you, man?" Sighs heavily to himself, shuffles to the window overlooking the school grounds. He can easily pick out Rhonnie because of her red hair. Watches her stepping up to the edge of the pool, then kneeling, waiting for Jin to pop his head up.

Jin remains underwater an unusually long time. The peace there swiftly evaporates above water. It's so hard to capture, harder than a dove. If only his lungs had no need for air, he'd stay at the bottom of the pool until his parents were ready to return to Japan. A floating hammock, the undulating aqua blue, white net of light, rocks him almost to sleep. But alas, he is human. He must breathe. Disappointed to leave his temporal nirvana, Jin floats motionless, as if lifeless, to the surface. A hand reaches his head and brushes through his water-matted hair. Shoji jabs him in the back with the rescue pole. Instinctually, he grabs that hand, arm, flips the unsuspecting, clothing-clad Rhonnie over his head into the water. Using her body's new inertia as leverage, he manages a kick. Three-quarters through the move, his eyes open to bright daylight, the first image, an overexposed picture of his foot enveloped in a sea of red hair. Too late to pull back, he can feel her skull against his curved arch and sole. Rhonnie hits the water, unconscious.

David, having stuck his head out the window to get a better look, bumps it against the wood above in shock. "Shit!"

Rhonnie sinks slowly downward, a torpedoed fishing boat. Chlorinated water enters her lungs. Jinshirou fills his with air and in two strong strokes plunges to Rhonnie. He nestles her head in his left arm, his left hand under the curve of her back. Holds her like a baby or a classical guitar. Her auburn hair coils in the water like the stripes of the American flag, like cattails in the autumn breeze. She is so peaceful, so very peaceful. With just the muscles of his thighs and calves, he thrusts gently once, twice, breaking the surface with his open mouth.

Carrying her from the water, laying her on the concrete, he turns her head to one side, presses his pulsing palm on her stomach and diaphragm. Water flows from her mouth like spilt flour from a bag. He tilts her chin up to the heavens, pinches her tall nose closed, then cups his lips around her full open mouth. Air from his lungs enters hers, then escapes. Air from his lungs enters her, then escapes. She coughs, convulses. Her body kicking moisture out through her throat. Finally, exhausted. She rests, once again peaceful. Too tired to move, eyes half drawn shut, sun smashing off them like atoms. She looks up in love at Jin's apologetic eyebrows. A subtle smile, too exhausted to be angry, she uses her precious little energy instead to run her hand along his pectorals. "Who are you?"

Jin exhales in relief, checks her head for a bump, then rolls over on his back beside her. Hearts racing, chests beating up and down, skins on taiko drums, they watch cloud reflections drift across the dorm windows.

David's been waiting, full uniform down to cleated shoes, helmet in hand. Jinshirou walks into the room with a towel around his damp swimsuit.

"What is with you man? You're wound way too tight."

"You have no right to be in the chamber!" Shoji scowls.

Jin does not respond, he opens his dresser in search of dry clothing. Listening for David's retreating footsteps, they don't sound. Still with his back to David. "No need to wolry about me."

David grabs the football off his bed. "I mean, I like you, but it's like there's something lurking inside you."

"*Lulrking?*"

Jinshirou dresses, David turns and looks out the window to give him some privacy. "Lurking? It's like, it's like, like something evi..."

Jinshirou, not really interested in the answer, interrupts, "Anyway, I'll not be back tonight."

"Rhonnie?" David chuckles, "Are you sleeping over there tonight?" He relaxes further thinking such an evening would serve well to unwind the taut Jin. "Because if you are... send Lucy over here."

But thoughts that ease David have the opposite effect on Jinshirou. "Be carleful how you say about-ew women."

"Yeah, right, I'll just keep my mouth shut and kick 'em in the head instead."

Jin finishes buttoning his shirt, steps into his shoes, grabs a small suitcase, an apple. He stabs a sharp look toward David. "You don't wolry about me."

Disappointed with Jinshirou's chosen distance, and insulted by Jin's glare, David shakes his head with a *forget you man* smile on his face as he steps out. "Whatever. Lock the door, I've got practice."

Across the quad, Lucy brushes her eyelashes black. "How do I look?"

Rhonnie smirks, "Great. I don't know why you're wasting it on Frank."

"Look who's talking. You're almost as beautiful as me, and you're gonna waste it on homework."

"You're right, but at least I asked him to the dance."

"Oriental guys don't like that."

"How would *you* know?"

"I know everything. I know all. So, whataya thinkin'? That Jin guy is just gonna show up one day and cash in his Veronica McKale napkin?"

Rhonnie sighs, "Get out of here." She picks up her history textbook, "Go dance with your QB. I've got a gallant hero awaiting me!"

Bright red grease smears across Lucy's lips. She kisses herself to smooth the spread, caps the stick, grabs her purse. "You sure you don't wanna come? That Ollie guy you used to like, he's gonna be there."

"*'Used to like'* is the operative phrase there. No, go, get out of here. Go have fun!"

"Don't worry about me you know. With a little luck, I won't be back tonight."

Rhonnie waves Lucy off, mumbles to herself, "With Frank's hormones, luck has nothing to do with it." She tosses the book onto her bed in disappointment. From under her pillow she pulls a bamboo flute, puts her lips to the blowhole, tries a tune. Warm air passes through, makes no tone.

Pre-dawn, Lucy removes her high heels, tiptoes into the dorm room. Rhonnie sleeps with her toy flute in one hand, history book in the other. Lucy is too tired to notice, falls into bed without undressing.

The gymnasium's double doors open startling a couple of stray cats. Arlen leads his four men onto the floor. The sun will rise soon. The rusty pond-blue sky only partially illuminates the huge room. The routines begin.

Arlen's man, Richard Spaddet shouts out, "Okay, right up! Make it perfect."

Denzel Grey pulls the creases from his pant legs. He marches onto an "X" taped on the floor. Somehow the wood sounds empty today, hollow. He looks down at the floor, and taps his foot one more time on the "X." The floorboards pop up from their secure lock, in a circle around him, a rope emerges from underneath. Like a clever snake, it slithers up his ankle and constricts, squeezes one word out of him, "Arlen!" Then the tug, so swift and unrelenting, topples Denzel in an instant. His head drops to the floor like the minute hand of an old dusty grandfather clock; the dim lights of the gymnasium blaze with the impact, then fade to blackness. A single rope laced over a rafter hoists the unconscious Denzel up to the ceiling. Jinshirou grips the other end of that rope. The counterweight, Jin descends in stealth from the ceiling as Denzel rises.

Jin ties the rope to a barbell as he lands on the gym floor. Three COIT members turn toward Jinshirou shocked, threatened, sweating. Arlen is frozen solid.

Richard, the most daring, nurses the adrenaline in his forearms, welcomes it to his chest which puffs in counter to the immediate cowardice he senses in his pals. "There's four of us and only one of him. And we've got guns."

Jimmy, hands out away from his gun, whispers to Richard, "Yeah, but no bullets."

Disgusted, probably propelled by Jimmy's cowering, Richard's gut churns into a steam engine, he lunges toward Jin like a locomotive. Jin, dispassionate, ever so comfortable to quarantine his emotions during a fight, leans gently to one side, the train that is Richard rushes by unable to correct trajectory. Jin can feel, smell, even see as infrared can detect heat, Richard's steaming hot Ki. Trained since the age of three, Jin raises his foot four inches to gently find Richards ankle as the freight passes. Richard's body snarls around his own Ki like tree branches in an avalanche. Richard crashes to the ground in a tangle, his eyes open in rage.

Jimmy breaks his freeze and runs to the door. "I'll get help!" He exits into the sunrise, relieved in the solace of something that is both cowardly and helpful.

Arlen is still frozen, as is Tad Decker just beside him. They stand like inverted icicles, silhouetted by the orange sun rising behind them, but do not melt. The same sun paints a bright red pepper edge across Jin's face as he marches confidently closer.

Richard unravels himself, wielding his rifle like a bat, he races up to Jin's back. Jin hears the whirring of the rifle's wooden butt as it rounds toward the back of his head. In the back of that head a dark cat leaps from a temple window nabbing a nimble bird in flight. Before the end of that thought, Richard's rifle is in Jin's hands. Richard looks down, lacerations in his palm begin to bleed. He looks up to see this mighty foreigner demonstrate with overwhelming accuracy, swiftness, and an acute lack of fear; how a rifle can be made to dance around the body of a human. Arlen had always been the best at this show of mastery. But then there was always the respect for the rifle. The fear of the rifle. But Jin makes mockery of the rifle, he knows without a second thought that he is much more deadly. They watch the rifle, a toothpick, a lilting piece of straw. The man, a burning arrow, a precisely targeted bolt of lightning.

Tad and Richard don't even see the butt coming. They don't hear it. The lightning flashes in their skulls upon impact. They seem to fall to the floor in one sweeping motion.

Arlen gasps, stands alone. Unable to move. Unable to make sense of his friends' falling, he did not see the impact either. He stares straight ahead, not at Jin, not at Tad and Richard, but at a space in the darkness that even he cannot pinpoint. A comfort in that darkness. He hears Jin chanting in Japanese, it seems to fit that darkness.

Before Arlen, Jin rolls an American flag onto the wooden floor. Jin steps on top of it, face to face he hugs Arlen. Arlen's body does not resist, only shakes, trembles. Jin hugs Arlen to his knees. The floor is cold on Arlen's knees, he begins to cry. Jinshirou draws Arlen's commander sword from its sheath. Jin kneels down behind Arlen, reaching the sword around to his front.

"You hold it!" Jinshirou commands.

Jin pulls Arlen's hands up to the sword's handle, its tip in Arlen's gut.

"You do it! Like Aro! Do it now!"

Arlen's trembles have become quakes. Jin has never seen this much fear in a man. Arlen's unrestrained fright almost shakes loose quarantined emotions within Jin. Compassion rattles inside its cage. But Jin has been trained well to suffocate the emotion. Jin's body holds Arlen, creates an unfettered conduit. Quaking resonates them both, a bio-cellular communication of fear from one living being to another. Compassion rattles, clanging noisily, threatens the completion of the mission, obscures the sound of Richard rolling back into consciousness.

"You do it! Like Aro! You do it now!"

Jin clenches his eyes closed tighter, seeks a reminder for his exact location in time, in this moment, purpose. He meditates, prays for a tormenting vision of Aro exploding, but none come to mind. Without effort Aro's hatred of America would bite into Jin's intestines, then many times daily the visions, without warning, play. But now, when they'd be of use, they are silent. Only the annoying clanging of mercy bumping against the bars of quarantine inside Jinshirou. He can feel the hinges clattering loose. He mentally tightens them, mentally forces a vision. He opens his mouth, reaches with his tongue to Aro's blood that is splattered on his face. The taste, he remembers that taste.

In one downward thrust, Jin's hands around Arlen's, the long narrow blade slides easily though Arlen's quivering torso. Arlen's blood spills onto the flag as his body falls toward it.

"No!" Richard's spirit escapes with his attempt to counterattack.

Jin raises to one knee. In hopes of calming his now angry compassion, he offers a silent prayer. But the peace, the release he expected does not come. Instead, the deafening rumble of his imprisoned mercy now echoes with the stomping feet of twenty-eight military students and officers approaching just one hundred feet from the building.

Jin stands, mission completed, he steps toward the rope. His hand reaches for it, but misses. He's confused. Tears refract his vision. Tears. He did not expect that.

Richard, too dizzy to stand, reaches for his ankle knife.

A splinter of sunlight fractures through Jin's tears, crackles like a streaming rainbow into his pupils. He wipes the rainbow away with his forearm. Jin's second grasp is successful. Rope in one hand, tight, coiled, he unties the barbell, bends his knees, leaps into a gentle ascension. Counterbalancing, Denzel's limp unconscious body descends to the floor.

Richard focuses, calms, aims, still on his back, jettisons his small knife at the gliding Jin. The blade finds Jin's left shoulder and sticks, stings like a rat bite, creates a heat, a fire that Jin uses to re-direct his attention. Mercy shuts up.

Jin takes to the darkness of the rafters, shuffles quickly to a small ceiling door, he slides it open. The unforgiving sun rushes into his eyes like water into Rhonnie's lungs. A flock of pigeons fly off in fear.

Richard scoots over to Arlen, rests his head on Arlen's chest, misses its pumping, covers the open belly with his hand, closes eyes, cries.

"I, I have seen action. I have seen men kill men. I have shot men from the sky. I have witnessed hell with my own eyes. It is a part of me I thought I'd sealed away tight. Far away, I never wanted to know it again. The men I've killed, and the friends I could not save. Their memories haunted me for years. I'd sealed it all away tight. In my old age, I even began to forget it ever happened." The Major stands at the SDFU stadium podium. His amplified voice bouncing, pounding the stands. Full as Homecoming game, the crowd is quieter than a bird.

Jinshirou hides anonymously next to Carlos and Skinner. Just two nights before, the place had been roaring with excitement. But now it grieves. No one grieved Aro -- not Shoji, not the boys at the temple -- only Jinshirou. How could all these people care about Arlen?

The Major pauses, stares down at the microphone in grief. A tear on the edge of his nose falls, his eyes narrow as he looks up into the blinding light of day. "But, Jesus Christ! This is South Dakota! This is my grandson! My family."

"Family" the word takes to the air like a missile. Like an ankle knife, it enters Jinshirou's ears, jagged edge first. A blood connection, a concept, a thought, communicated by a man's vocal cords vibrating, mouth shaping, microphone converts the dance to electricity, circuit to speaker, compressions of air through distance, eardrums stutter, transmit through nerve impulses to Jinshirou's brain, acknowledges, accepts, understands, then almost without permission erupts into a million biological elements that search Jinshirou's anatomy and find without the lapse of time a cage of barred emotions. The key turns.

Arlen's mother painfully finds the podium. "Um," She wipes tender red eyes. "I know this was supposed to be a celebration. Arlen was supposed to lead the Hawks. But, but..." She pauses, sniffles, "And I didn't have to get up here. They told me just to go home. But, I know." Her voice strengthens. "*I know!* Whoever did this. Whoever did... you did not know Arlen. And now I'm going to tell you. Because I know you're here." Her worn emaciated eyes scour the stands. "Or you're watching." They pierce the TV cameras. "And you are not going to get away with this... not without knowing, Arlen was a good man. A damn good man. Quality. Sincere. He gave me pride. He helped his brother finish high school. He used to help me cook. He washed my hair when I broke my hip. He used to wash my hair! I loved that boy! And now you, a person that has no idea about love -- only some sick demented revenge... Whatever you're angry about, whatever would make you kill somebody... it wasn't Arlen's fault! You killed the wrong man!" Now through gritted teeth, "I will hunt you down. I will find you and I will stab you with Arlen's memory. You killed the wrong man. You are the evil one." Arlen's mother's pupils reach out, scratch the pain of onlookers.

The key turns. Jin holds head down, palms to back of skull. Why did it never occur to him that Arlen had a mother?

A university police officer takes the microphone. "This, this is not easy for any of us. I like to think we are family here at SD. And Arlen was a big brother to a lot of us." The officer opens a small sheet of paper, takes a breath, "So, well, you all know that Arlen was found slain early this morning over in Aug's Gymnasium. We have witnesses who believe that the assailant was an Asian male about six foot, and because of some rituals that were performed, it is very likely that he is Japanese. The assailant also sustained a knife wound to the left arm." The officer pauses for another breath, "That's it, gang. That's what we know. So, if you have any information for us. You can... ah... bring it to the COIT office or Campus Security."

Strikingly sad, the school President takes the microphone. "Let's have a moment of silence for Arlen J. Williams and return to our classes."

The key turns. Jinshirou tries to stop his tears, he cannot. Eyelids clench as tight as Aro's grip had been. Jinshirou cowardly prays that tears streaming outside his face won't stain public his guilt inside.

The key turns. Quarantine shatters like crystal, emotions splatter like Aro's blood. The internal airtight cage implodes. Guilt, insecurity, shame, scatter like bubbles. Swim through veins, crawl through skin, pry through eyelids. The tears refuse surrender. Pry open eyes. Shame expects punishment. Guilt expects one thousand fingers at one dirty soul. But instead, Jin is lost in a sea of crying faces: white, black, brown, yellow, red, tan. His rescue raft of anonymity quickly capsizes in the ocean of painful tears. With no quick punishment to distract, Jin begins a sincere grieving for the death of his own soul.

Rhonnie's red hair floats amidst the waves, rocking through the crowd toward Jin.

Students slowly file out of the stadium. Jinshirou looks to the flags on the top bleachers. American flag rolls out in the wind, for the first time does not reveal Aro bleeding for Jin. Japanese flag swinging, red ball bursts with Arlen's blood until the entire flag is dripping.

"Jinshirou!" Rhonnie finds Jin empty. "This is too weird. This is just too weird."

Jinshirou still staring at the flag through puddled eyes. "Disglrace on my country."

"Don't do that. Come on, it's not your fault." Rhonnie waits a full minute for Jin's response, it never comes. She bites her lip, checks her watch. "Well, I've got to get back. My folks are driving in to pick me up. Jin, stop by before you go, would you?"

Jin stares quietly at the flags, ash burnt light rushes in through his kaleidoscope eyes. He doesn't move. Doesn't respond. Rhonnie hugs his arm, then turns away with a mix of feelings she doesn't have enough information or time to understand.

People bleed from the stadium to the parking lot. Jinshirou lingers, alone, staring at the flag. Nausea finally finds him and he rushes to the men's room. Slamming the stall door, he kneels before the toilet, lifts the lid, heaves with all his might, silently wishing all of his insides will wash their way out of his mouth. The vomit flows thick, abrasive as bricks, though not a single organ escapes. Jinshirou drops his head on the cold porcelain commode. Empty, vomited hollow.

"Hey Yingyang, Pearl Harbor not enough for ya?"

Jinshirou's head ducks even lower. He listens quietly.

A COIT fellow and a few other angry friends of Arlen circle around an Asian kid at a urinal. Under the stall door, Jin sees their feet.

"What?" the Asian kid zips up. "Hey, I'm not Japanese. I'm Chinese, dude."

"Close enough." One in the group responds. Another tears the sleeve of the innocent student.

"See! No knife wounds." The Chinese kid happily reports.

Drawing a knife. "Shame, we'll have to make our own."

A single drop of blood drops to the white floor just in front of Jin's stall. An unsettling quiet echoes. Polished shoes shuffle out. Jin swallows, mercy arm-wrestles fear, compassion takes on guilt, opens the stall door. On the floor, doubled over, bleeding from the forearm and neck, the Chinese kid grimaces in pain. Jin finds the torn sleeve, wraps the wound.

"I'm Chinese." The boy blurts in anger and pain, "Fucking Japanese killed my ancestors too!"

"You okay," Jin comforts, "You be okay."

Jin sticks his head out to the hall. "Help! My flriend is hurt!"

Two security guards run in as Jin runs out.

South of the stadium, Ollie grabs David, shoves him against a bulletin board.

"Dude?" David spits out in surprise, "What is your problem?"

"You!" Ollie's eyes sharpen with suspicion. "You're tall. You're Japanese."

David, stunned, shakes his head. "Ollie, take it easy man. Relax. It's me, David. Look, no knife wounds."

Ollie looks at David's left arm, then grimaces, "You're still Japanese."

"Jesus, Ollie! So is your CD player!"

Ollie looks up, not knowing where to put his anger, not committing to let it go, either.

"What are you gonna do?" David reclaims ownership of his arm, "check all your friends?" He reaches in Ollie's backpack and throws Ollie's CD player against the wall. "There you go, check that for knife wounds too!"

In the University security office SDFU security debrief Arlen's COIT pals for the third time.

Red-faced, eyes teary, Richard speaks through heavy breaths, "I don't know, he just took off through the roof, the fuckin' bastard." Richard's eyes flood. "My God, why Arlen?"

Though he's heard the story ten times already, the security officer sniffs up his wet nostrils, determined to maintain a professional debriefing. "It was his left arm you got?"

"Yeah," Richard barks back, exhausted with the repitition, "his left arm!"

Detective White, a black man in his late fifties, steps into the room briskly. He's been rushing around campus looking for this office. All eyes turn to him.

"I'm Detective White, Sioux Falls P.D." White flashes his badge. "Sorry for your loss, boys. It's not pretty, I know, and now it's my job to catch this guy. Sounds like you've all been doing some good preliminary work."

"Sir, Officer Jenkins here," University Security introduces himself, "We're just about finished talking with these men. We're happy to have your help."

"Great, then you boys take a break, leave us your cell-phone numbers, go home, visit your loved ones," White nods at Richard and Arlen's men. "We'll handle it from here."

Richard gets up anxiously. "Somebody better *handle* it." He mutters as he leaves.

Jenkins waits until the four have left the office. "Sir, Records Department just gave us the list of students with Japanese sounding last names."

"I just need six footers." White switches immediately into problem solving mode.

"Yeah, we got it down to fifty students that way…"

"Fifty?"

"And then we went ahead and pulled the files of the most recent transferees. Got one kid straight from Japan two weeks ago."

"All right, great. I'm impressed. Let's take the top five, split them up. I want to know parents' names, dorm room numbers, addresses, classmates. Then let's get our asses out there."

David storms into his dorm room. Without hesitation, he attacks Jin's special little corner, rips open the small drawer. The picture of Aro's charred mother falls out.

"Jesus Christ!" David cries to himself. He slams his forehead forward into his palms, shakes his head. Jin enters behind him.

David turns his teary eyes from the photo to Jin. "What? Did you think this would make up for your grandmother?"

"Not *my* grandmother."

"Yeah, whatever! Your mother, your aunt, your fucking cousin's second wife." David's tears begin to flow unabated. "Jesus Christ!" He coughs out a laugh of disgust, *"Don't forget Nagasaki?"* He turns to see Jin's eyes. "That's history, dude! You can't nail it on Arlen! It wasn't his fault! He wasn't anywhere near it."

Jin is silent.

"What are you gonna do, kill all these fucking Americans because sixty years ago, they blew up your aunt Keiko?" David stands up, he shoves his chest forward. "Then fucking cut my guts out!" He pulls his shirt up. "Because I'm a fucking American too!"

Still Jin is silent. This is just a small taste of the punishment he craves.

"Jesus Christ, he was innocent! He wasn't even born!" David waves the photograph, sadistically. "Did it do it for you? Did it get your rocks off? Did it bring this woman back to life?" David crumples the photo, throws it into Jin's face.

"Or, let me guess, you did it for Japan. Like Japan gives a shit! Did you do it for the Japanese? ... Yeah? Let me tell you something, you big dumbfuck! ... My best friend searches my body for knife wounds. *My best fuckin' friend*!"

With one strong angry arm, David swings his repugnance into Jin's shrine. It topples and scatters like a deck of cards.

Jin stands dumbfounded. Wanting to cry, but stupidly too proud to cry in front of David's Japanese face. Jin deflects the pressure, runs out of the building to Rhonnie's dorm room.

Rhonnie, at her window, watches as chaos overtakes the campus. Her door opens, Jin steps in.

Peacefully powerless and sad. Rhonnie turns toward him. "I'm glad you came." She hugs Jin, lays her head on his chest.

"I killed him."

The small sentence stabs at Rhonnie's hopeful calm. She tilts her head up slowly. "What?" She whispers so softly she wishes Jin will not hear, not explain.

But Jin will show no mercy to her calm. "Thse COIT boy, I killed him."

"It's not true. Not you. You're good."

Jinshirou rolls up his sleeve and looks away from the bloodstained bandage in shame. "I thsought... Aro. Thzey killed Aro." Jin slides from Rhonnie's hug to the floor. "Thzey blew him up. I tasted-ew Aro, his brlood fell in my mouss, Aro's mothzer... Tar…"

Rhonnie closes her eyes, holds her ears, shakes her head, lowers to the floor also. Begins to pound on his chest. "No! No! No!"

"I thsought loyalty. I, I thsought unity. Brlothzerhood."

As Jin slips from Rhonnie's comforting arms into the comfort of his own confession, Rhonnie fist fights the realization, longs for the man of whom she'd spent the last days daydreaming.

Lucy stomps in. "Jin! Are you all right? It's crazy out there. I'm afraid for you. They're beating up Oriental guys all over the place. I heard they chased one off the history building. That guy died! I'm worried about you, Jin... maybe we should go with you and get you outta here?"

Jinshirou shakes his head, crying, "My blrothzers pay in brlood... again! Dis time, my fault. Not Aro's... not-ew Amerlica's fault. Mine."

He kisses Rhonnie on the head, slips from her punches, from Lucy's concern.

Dusk befalls SDFU Main Square like dust. A group of angry White, Latino and Black students push around another Asian guy.

"You're a big gook, even a fucking martial arts student. Let's see you take on twenty of us."

"I do not. I did not. I Vietnamese!"

The mob presses, forces the martial arts student to fight. The student kicks and blocks with great speed, but is overpowered by the twenty in less than one minute. They hold him belly up, Jimmy draws the knife.

"It not me! It not me!" The struggling young man screeches for his life, the soft last sound a gazelle makes at the sight of a charging lion.

The knife catches a flash of the last light of day. Jimmy's head catches a sharply thrown acorn. The nut small, pain quick, acute, Jimmy's angst ejects from his body in exchange for confusion, momentary blindness. His knees buckle, knife drops from hand.

The mob looks along the path of the projectile, finds Jinshirou cloaked in black, a Ninja in the tree above.

Jimmy becomes cognizant, remembers his thrust to kill a crying man only three seconds prior. Three seconds later, gratitude for the stinging pain in his temple. Gratitude that the knife is in the dirt, not in the man's heart.

The cloaked Jin speaks, "Do no hate eberly one of us for somesing only I am responsibrle. Hate me. Thzey look-ew like me, but don't know anysing of killing... like me."

Jin removes his mask. "Half-ew centulry of anger brlought two innocent-ew people to die. If you must anglry -- dilrect your anglry to me."

Richard has one hand on the Vietnamese kid, one eye up at Jin. Tempering his anger with a moment's pause he shouts, "Show me the knife wound!"

"Does dis carlm your doubt?" Jin flicks Richard's knife at the mob. The knife sticks in the ground just inches from Richard's clutch.

Denzel grabs the knife from the ground. "That's your fucking knife, man!"

Someone in the mob grabs a knife of their own and flings it through the twilight, through the veiling leaves to Jin. It's a good throw, dead on target, but Jin snatches the knife from the air. This simple feat quiets the mob. With their complete attention, Jinshirou raises the blade to his own head. It's cold. It's jagged. But that feels right. Feels just. Jin presses the sharp edge into his skull. A trickle of blood. A patch of skin, scalp and hair fall from his forehead to the ground. "Now you can know... the guirlty one. If you hate me, don't make-ew yourselb like me. Don't kill somebody because-ew thzeir skin is my color. Because-ew thzeir eyes-ew are my shape."

Rhonnie cannot find reason to leave the floor. She's a strong woman, she's answered her fair share of life's blows with a pair of fighting fists. She never collapsed, but the sum, the cumulative effect of those hardships gang up on her now. Unrelated past pains find one another inside her body. Like beads of mercury, they bleed through her arteries connecting together. Her bones and flesh are no match for the weight of liquid metal.

Lucy runs her hands through Rhonnie's red curls in hopes of comforting her.

Through Rhonnie's cracked door, Jinshirou's bleeding head peaks one last time. Little Aro peers through his parents' bedroom door. Aro's mother on her knees, broken in tears after a beating from Aro's father.

Jinshirou's tears mix with the blood from his head wound, stream to the floor. Lucy shudders at the diluted mixture creeping in from the hallway.

"I am solry. So solry. I wish-ew to bring him back. I wish-ew to bring sem bosth back. I wish-ew to kill Aro twice."

"You're a killer, a murderer. I don't know you." Rhonnie's face still buried in her hands. "I thought, I thought I loved you."

Jin slinks over to the huge window as if it were a painting of the campus. His sins lacquer broad strokes of red. Jin drops his forehead to the pane of glass and adds to the art with streaks from his face, eyes shut in shame. "You did."

The three remain silent save for whimpers. Jinshirou's eyes open, police walk from the street to dorm entrances below. He pulls his head away from the window in a dizzy fear. The sharp movement blackens the day for an instant. But only an instant, though faint, Jin remains conscious, despite wishing otherwise. Despite welcoming that blackness, despite longing for black out. The police see him through the bloodied glass, they quicken their steps. Jinshirou stumbles to the sink, he rinses his face with water, but the self-inflicted wound makes more blood. Opening a nearby cabinet, he searches for bandages, grabs a maxi pad, wraps it on his head with a nylon stocking.

"Veronica McKale?" Detective White knocks on the door, still ajar.

Rhonnie remains on the floor, weeping.

"Is he here?" Opens the door slowly, gun drawn, step careful.

Rhonnie looks up, face streaking with tears. "I don't know him."

White and crew search the small room.

"He was here, but he's gone." Lucy's voice has gone flat, too confused to choose an emotion.

Jin's mother chops raw chicken. The TV flickers behind her. "Well, again, today's top story -- a tragedy. Earlier this morning, the outstanding young cadet, Arlen Williams, was murdered on SDFU grounds. The assailant mutilated the victim over a United States flag. This horrible slaying appears to have been a payback for Nagasaki, one of the two Japanese cities destroyed by US A-bombs that ended World War Two. Police are asking for your help. The suspect is around 6 foot, Japanese, wounded in the left arm, and well-versed in some martial arts. If you hav..."

With the tip of her blade, Jin's mom switches off the set. She drops the knife on the cutting board, leans against the wall, silently sobs. Jin's father steps into the room with a seriousness that has never found his face prior. He hugs his wife, they slide to their knees in mourning.

Jin stands among bristly bushes alongside the borrowed house. The splintered branches prick his legs through his pants as he peers through the window at his broken parents.

Arlen's mother's cry echoes from the stadium to the neighborhood, rings without regard to duration. The angry howl of the atom bomb echoes against the hills surrounding Nagasaki.

Sirens approach.

Jin lays two dozen roses on the doorstep, turns away into the dusk, into the echoes, into amber waves of shame.

The bright late morning sunlight burns Jin's eyes open. As bright as yesterday's momentary black outs were dark, as white as the spark that tore apart Aro. It's not a pure white. It's not a virginal white, rather a burning white, a blinding white. Jinshirou bobs his cracked crown like a blind man, searches for a sense of surroundings. Traffic clamor drives from below. The city, but where are the buildings? Birds so near, a choir of pigeons only feet away. A ledge blurs into view, vertigo, rooftops roll beyond the ledge. On the ledge, a bloodied maxi pad. Jin raises his hand to his head, he does not recall removing the stocking. Stuck in the pad, a needle threaded and trailing to a spool. Jin stumbles to get up. A throbbing rushes to his skull. He reaches to hold the pain. But instead of clasping an open wound, or even a bandaged wound, a coarse weave scratches against his thumb. Stitches. There, near the corner of the flat rooftop, a broken piece of mirror, crawls to it, examines himself. Stitches indeed. The wound is sewn shut. Jin checks his arm, also sewn, that wound.

"Ah, I see you have wakened up." Silitei, a well-groomed, but not well-dressed, little black man hobbles, from the corner.

"Did you do thzis?" Jin points to his wound.

"I don't know who did that, but I sewed it up!" Silitei smiles disarmingly.

"You do not look like-ew a doctolr."

"Yes, well in Kenya I was a street tailor." Silitei spreads his arms proudly in the air to show off his apparel sewn and re-sewn many times, as patched as a quilt. "Do you like my work?"

Jin squints his blurried eyes. Aro spreads his arms, revealing a belly ribbed with dynamite and a smile as blinding as the day's first light.

Jin shudders, "I will go."

"Go where? No, bwana, I don't know what happened to you, but you bled. You need to rest more. Sit down. Here, I brought up some food -- chakula!"

Silitei hops over an A/C vent to a cardboard box. He drops it upside down between them, from his pocket pulls a wrapper of leftover French fries, a half-eaten burger, a cob of corn with at least two rows of kernels left. "You Americans have this funny yellow corn. I'm still not used to it."

"I do not eat-ew hamburger."

"And I don't like yellow corn. But that's what we got, now eat." Silitei grimaces, "If I'd known you'd be such a whiner, I might should have let you bleed to death."

Jin remembers his manners, his parents' manners, his parents' upbringing. "Forgib me. Sank you." He picks up the hamburger, it's cold, soggy, the bread is powdered and stiff, but the scent of food ignites his hunger. Confusion dissipates, hunger howls. Jin savors the small morsel, someone else's leftovers. In a matter of quiet minutes the food is gone. Jin sighs and looks up at his host. "Kenya?"

Silitei, unhappy with the ignorance of his guest, spanks the box back up and puts it away. "In Africa, man! *You Americans!* All you know of the world is your own backyard! Kenya, man! East Africa."

"I am Japanese."

"Yeah, so what?" Silitei throws the empty cob on the ground. "I'm still hungry!"

Sugar takes to his blood, Jin's eyes become suddenly focused, suddenly very present. They target the little Kenyan street tailor. "Why?" Jin maintains his stare. "Why did you mend me?"

"You were bleeding."

Like a thirty-foot wave, like the rush of the morning's white light, the present, the actual present befalls Jin. All his life, up to this very moment, Jin had been stitched tightly to the past. Not his own past, but someone else's torn, sad, tortured past. This little Kenyan tailor with the patched sweater, dulled glossy eyes, mender of his wounds, broke every last stitch of Aro's hatred with three words. Sutures torn, so fall several layers of past. Remains Jin's present. At great cost. Remains Jin's present. Assumed American, unselfish assistance received.

Absolute present.

Jin smiles. Perhaps for the first time in his life the smile comes from the heart. From the heart, a place he'd never been taught to study. Mother had some idea of that place, but she always seemed so weak. From the heart, a smile rises.

"Yeah, so what? You were bleeding, man, and I am still hungry!"

The smile widens, Jin's eyes close. He listens. He can hear the wind circle in the corner where the side ledges meet. He can hear the traffic below, hear Silitei breath. With a sharp swift turning lunge, Jin grasps a pigeon as it slows to land on the ledge.

Silitei's tired eye's light up. "You eat doves in Japan, too!"

Jinshirou laughs at himself. "Some people do."

"Come." Silitei helps Jin to the other side of the roof. He picks up a small rusted grill. "In Kenya, we call this a *jiko*."

Nervous, David knocks on Rhonnie's dorm room door. No answer, thinking for several minutes, he tries the knob. The door opens.

Rhonnie has the chair up to the blood-stained window. She's sitting with her back to David, doesn't move as he enters.

"You alright?"

Still with her back to him, Rhonnie shakes her head *no*. David's eyes close in empathy. The campus teamed with anger, violence, confusion just one day before. Now it is still. Quiet. Deathly settled. Ronnie grasps the arms of the chair, pushes herself up, turns to David. Dried streams of tears layer her freckled face, now drained rivers on eroded desert landscape.

Bones and feathers litter the rooftop. Jin and Silitei chew on charcoal grilled pigeons as another three roast on the jiko.

"These birds are very good." Silitei pats his belly. "I'm glad I found you."

Jin smiles back. Despite the plump kindness of a rooftop vagabond and a solid night's sleep, Jin falls tired.

Silitei, still with a mouthful, jumps toward a pigeon sidestepping along the ledge. The bird flies off, Silitei watches it disappear into the sky. "Japanese man, you've got to teach me how to do that." Hearing no response, Silitei turns away from the sky to find Jin fast asleep. "Yes, of course. Not now. Not now, it's better that you sleep."

Wrapping the rest of the fresh food in plastic bags, Silitei stores them away in the cardboard box.

He then spreads yesterday's newspapers over Jinshirou. **"Three Slain in SDFU"** the headline reads, but Silitei doesn't notice, nor would it matter, as he cannot read.

"You sleep. And you know what, bwana? My belly's so full, I think I won't be awake too much either."

The two foreigners lay where they'd eaten. Dead birds that had flown only hours earlier digest in their stomachs. The dusk sprinkles over the two new roof mates, and then the night with the might of darkness. By midnight, Orion has rotated far up into the Southern sky. Jinshirou awakens. Moonlight glows like a ghost beyond the newspaper that covers his face. **"Arlen dead at 22"** The headline handcuffs Jin's painful past to his recently discovered present.

Jin sadly, silently stands, covers Silitei with the leftover papers, steps toward the fire escape down. Pauses for one last look at sleeping Silitei, a sad smile rises from his heart. "In Japan, we call it *hibachi*."

The night drapes like a thick fleece blanket over the city of Sioux Falls. Though the days are wrought with anguish, hatred, grief, the night fleece muffles all. This three AM feels like any other three AM. In the morning, the mourning resumes.

Safe from the news, safe from judgement, Silitei wakes atop his chosen building. The problems at street level may as well be the problems of another country. His new Japanese friend flown, Silitei remembers him with a quick lunge toward a much faster pigeon. He smiles, laughs.

From the street below, Jin cocks his neck up toward Silitei's rooftop, watches the fast bird fly.

Two people sit at the bus stop, one reads the newspaper, holds it high like a sign, a poster, a mirror for Jin. His graduation picture stares back. Frozen by the image of himself, of a purer self, an innocent self, Jin lets his own photo judge. A patrol car pulls up to the corner and breaks Jin's reflection. He turns his face away from the police, away from his younger face. Pulls a baseball cap over his stitches, they sting. With a hidden step, Jin walks directly out of town, dodging the occasional lingering glances.

The crowds thin as Jin approaches the Falls. He rinses his face and continues further up river where no citizens walk. In the brush, Jin disrobes. Submerges, slides into the river. His body hot with regret, does not cool in the chilling water. A small cloud of steam mists above the surface where he hopes to cleanse himself. But only the sweat is taken down stream.

Finishing, dressed, walking the American Indian paths. Nearing a small town, a party of children jump into the river from the branch of a tree.

"Come on, Henry. Just do it!"

"Okay, here goes!" Henry shouts. His eyes gleam with excitement. His heart rate increases with the dare, the fun, the splash.

Unabashed innocence hits Jin like a cinderblock, like a brick aimed directly at his wounded head. Without filtering, his first instinct -- hate the child for being so pure. Purity seems to mock. It's only purpose to dig, to remind Jin of his sins. But Jin is no stranger to disciplined thought.

"Look at me. I hate dis chilrd?" Jin grips his own ears. "Why? He is beautiful. I am ugrly. I hate me. Applropriate choice, I hate me, not dis chilrd. He is innocent." Jin closes his eyes. "Can I not see him beautiful without feelring my own repulse?"

Jin opens his eyes. Henry's friend dives headfirst. The water splashes up into the sun, sparkling like daytime fireflies, the flames of a hundred splintered candles. It is clearly a radiant, awe-inspiring sight. Jin knows it should be, but no awe, no inspiration. It takes all of Jin's attention just to stop blaming the children for his own loss of pride, gain of shame.

Steps away, cries for himself, unnoticed. The cool dirt path feels good beating against this callous soul's callused soles. Legs tire, but Jin continues in hope of punishing his body.

Past this small town, and another, far into the woods, a car is parked. Inside a man and a woman feverishly kiss in the back seat. Their clothes drape haphazardly, on and off, revealing, not revealing, touching, sweating. The car rocks back and forth. Jin is stopped by the sight of them through steamed windows. As if waiting for him, camouflaged in a tree, cupid sends a burning arrow of jealousy straight through Jinshirou's heart.

Jin reaches into his shirt pocket, pulls out a wrinkled napkin. There's a hole in it where the arrow passed. He rereads the scratched English: "Rain Check. Good for one dance with the lovely Veronica McKale."

Poolside, Rhonnie runs her hands down Jin's six-packed stomach.

Heavy breaths from the car disturb Jin's peaceful memory.

"Verlonica McKale, so solry."

Jin continues his walk, his excursion, deviation, escape from reality. His neck loosens into mud, his boulder head hunches, struggles to stay atop his wet clay spine. His sagging branch arms hang low in their sockets.

Laughing, coughing, smoking distract his self-punishment. Three teens sit in a clearing passing a paper-rolled stick of marijuana.

Billy grimaces to hold the fumes in his lungs, they break through his nose in spurts.

Bored to tears and unimpressed with his high, Dan points at the train tracks. "Dude, I heard that if you, like, cut one of these massive wires by the tracks, then you can, like, make those crossing things come down."

Billy passes the joint. "Crossing gates?"

Dan nods. "Yeah, those will come down and, like, just stay down."

Jason laughs, "Causing massive confusion."

Billy nods repetitively, his neck extending like an ostrich. "Cool."

The dirty wet smell of pine and burnt leaves wafts past. Jin turns his head, moves along. The balls of his feet make no sound, his legs break no sticks.

A bobcat kitten paws at a toad. Jin steps to get a closer look. Mother bobcat steps behind Jin to get a closer look. Jin suddenly, silently stops. The sharp-edged stare of the protective mother stabs through Jin's back. He feels it lodged into his ribcage, next to cupid's arrow of jealousy. The moment freezes, like the Falls in winter, like drips into icicles. Will the weighted ice spear through him? Will the bobcat attack?

A clanging alarm shatters the icicle, the kitten runs off in surprise. The toad, lucky with random freedom, hops fast into the stream. Jin turns to face mother bobcat. Horns blare. With a disapproving breath, a soft hiss of disgust, mother's stare fractures, she follows after the young one.

Invisible, the whirling ringing whistles through the branches and trees. Like the squirrels and birds, Jin scurries. The once welcome ground now rumbles below his feet. His conscious conscience measures the shear weight of fear. Sometimes as light as a dove, sometimes as heavy as a locomotive. Sometimes clasping like the claws of a cat, and at still others, just as fleeting.

Aro picks a fallen rod of bamboo from the forest floor. He waits patiently until all the bees have retreated into the hive, then with one swift motion, he strikes it with the stick. In an instant, a dust-devil of bees swells. As if one being, they pulse. The boys scatter. Aro only smiles, his eyes shine up at the bees, delight as if a sunset. A six-year-old Shoji pushes away from seven-year-old Jin, who freezes in fear. A few bees sting Jin's trembling flesh, but the bulk seek out the fastest running - Shoji. Though guilty, though inches from the hive, Aro has not a single sting.

Jin slows his step.

"They will find the one among you who runs the fastest away."

Jin pauses, lets the animals rush by. Alone now, only with the insects and plants, Jin focuses, listens. The alarm, behind, is not a siren, not a whistle. But a bell, a quick ringer. A horn also, perhaps several. The vibrations below his feet, the tremble of the Earth, the earlier smell of burnt pine. Sans the cloud of fear, Jin finally pieces the puzzle together. He turns one hundred and eighty degrees, runs top speed toward the alarm that had only seconds before sent him scurrying in fear.

"Run toward that which causes you fear."

The cover of trees gives way to a twenty foot clearing many miles long. Train tracks. One-quarter mile in the direction of the bells, a crossing gate blocks traffic in both directions. No train in sight, impatient drivers honk. A daring soul here and there darts around the red/white wooden arms.

Jin finds a pole near the tracks. Like a bee on a string, a broken wire hangs sparking in the light breeze against the pole. Restless motorists lose their patience, now drive around the gates in a steady stream.

Jin dips back into the trees, returning with some strong vine. Wrapping his hands with his shirt for insulation, he ties the stripped cable back together with the vine. Mended metal. Immediately the gates rise. The bells arrest. The horns stop. The traffic flows as normal.

Jin pulls back into his shirt, walks along the tracks away from the crossing. A pinpoint ball of white sways between the trees ahead. The ground vibrations increase their amplitude. Jin pauses, turns, squints back at the gates now over half a mile behind. They are silent, tall. The ball of white shimmers with the heat of the engine. It slowly dilates, wavers left and right with the rock of the train in the tracks. Jin again squints at the gates, the silent tall gates. His heart beat increases to the frequency of ground vibrations. Like a sprinter, he fires from a freeze, rushes toward the cable. The freight train now thunderous in sound, blaring in horn, chases.

The fastest runners can finish a mile in four minutes. Though strong, electric within ten or twenty feet, Jin will need more than two and a half minutes for one half mile. The quarter mile to the cable will take a little over a minute.

Wind rushing through his hair, black and red scar leading, so much capacity for thought, limitless imagination behind that scar. His abilities to think, find solutions are sharpened, well trained, but in his mind only plays a comparison. He remembers the fear that came with the ringing and blaring. And now the silence of the gates. Alarm, but no need. And now, need, but no alarm. In his head time pauses in irony, but outside, time clicks by at the rate of one second per one second. The train is in plain view behind him, but traffic still swims the crossing.

As if impressed with Jin's sprint alone, the quiet gates lower, the bells clanging erupt, traffic stops. Jin calms his pace passes the cable, which is still strapped tight. He continues ahead to ensure the warning remains in place. Cars ahead, people. Scores of innocent people. The freight train slowly passes Jin. Its weight, its mass, its apathy feel good in the manner with which it eclipses Jin's own mass and weight. Jin pushes his step to equal the speed of the train then leaps into the darkness of an open cargo door.

"Hey buddy, this is my box car!" A grizzly man, unkempt, smelling of liquor grumbles, eyebrows at an angry angle. The man jumps up with a stick and points it at Jin, now lying on the dirt dust grit wooden floor of the train.

"Bockas car?"

A B-29 flies past the passenger airliner. The metal shimmers in the sunlight, the words "Box Car" painted across its side. The grizzly, unkempt pilot connects eyes with Jin. He mouths, "I'm sorry ... I thought..."

Jinshirou stands, grabs the stick from the smelly man and in one motion pins him against the floor. Stick to his neck, head hanging out of the open door in the unforgiving twilight and loud breeze, the man stammers for a new angle. "I'm sorry... I thought you were somebody else," He coughs, "It's a big car, I can share it."

The man searches for mercy in Jin's distant eyes. Finally, the eyes become less distant.

With the pilot's head dangling from the cockpit, Jinshirou watches the small object free fall, patches of landslide underneath like a carpet, buildings begin to populate the carpet, until the object strikes the largest gathering.

The stick, bark whittled away, begins to collapse the man's Adam's Apple. Now choking, gasping, "I'm sorry. I didn't mean it."

The horrid smell of old whiskey and vomit break into Jin's head. They crash the image of an airplane. Erase the backdrop of Japan at five thousand feet and replace it with South Dakota at five.

Jin relaxes back. Tosses the stick out the door. Pulls the unkempt man back into the car. The man rolls on his back, fills his lungs with air, calms enough to wipe the dirt from the front of his coat. The man giggles, then laughs, then finds his bottle under the garbage, takes a sloppy swig, then giggles some more.

Jin speaks, "I forgib you."

The man rubs his neck. "For what?"

Swallowed in the belly of the train, rocking, relentless clanging of metal to rail, meticulous clicking of tracks connected at precise intervals, heavy boxes chained together, Jin's sleep has been as heavy as the engine. He wakes at dawn, jumps from the train into Black Hills.

Hungry, it's been a day and a half since he'd feasted on birds, and thirsty, Jin begins his hike, now listening for a stream. In short time, he can hear it bubble, smell it... even taste the fish. Legs bent into a squat, Jin brings the water to his mouth. He rinses some roots he'd dug up on the way and begins to nibble them. An eighth of a mile downstream a father teaches his son to fly fish. Jin watches, nibbles. He remembers his father, but cannot recall any moments. Father and son. He can remember his father coming home from work, patting his head, watching TV, but what did he ever learn from his father? Only Aro. When he learned as a boy from an older man, it was always Aro.

"Hey! Hey, you!"

Jin, startled, looks up from the water. He's long since finished the roots. The shadows have shortened, the son is upon him.

The boy stands knee deep in the stream. "Hey, you hungry?"

Regaining his sense of time and relative safety. "You sink I look hunglry?"

"What? Sort of. Anyway, we cooked way too many fish. You want one?" The boy paws up a cleaned and fried rainbow trout.

The edge of the sun dashes off the dreamy stream, skipping like stones into Jin's eyes which suddenly flow of tears. Not prepared to cry in front of the child, Jin lowers his head, hides his wet cheekbones. But indeed, the boy is right. Hungry. Jin reaches out his hand, takes the fish.

"Sank you. You are kind."

"Ain't too many rainbow trout here in the Black Hills. We got lucky, yeah. Ouch, what happened to your head? My dad says you don't have to be ashamed to cry if you're really hurt." The boy rolls his sleeve back. "I cried like a little boy when I cut this arm here."

To not look at the boy's wound would be impolite, so Jin dares to show his teary eyes; the light dances through them like the stream itself.

"But don't cry when you're not really hurt, that's what my dad says. That's just being a baby." The boy spanks his wound. "Five stitches. But look, it's all healed now."

The boy turns toward his father downstream; he hops through the water splashing it into a spray. White light refracts in the mist, splitting into waves of red, orange, yellow, green, blue, indigo and violet.

Jin chews into the fish. "Rainbow tlrout in Brlack Hills."

Hat tightly over scar, Jin stands before Mount Rushmore. Four proud faces look out and over him unconcerned, unmoved by his emotions. Apathetic to his hatred, his murder. Uncaring of Aro or Arlen. Faces of stone, all they seem to express is pride. Pride and strength.

Bustling with tourists from every country, Jin once again welcomes anonymity. He asks a white person, "Who are dese men?"

"Sorry, no English... German." The man answers.

"Washington, Jefferson, Lincoln and Roosevelt," the man's friend responds with a slight German accent.

"Roosebelt?"

Impressed and awed with this work, the German man continues, "Yes, can you believe the artist was inspired enough to spend his life carving it?"

"Why?"

"Why? Who knows? *These Americans*," he smiles, "they get an idea in their heads, they're gonna try it. Carving up a mountain -- you have to respect that, don't you?"

"Roosebelt?"

"Yeah, Roosevelt. And another thing, the artist died before he finished. His son finished. His son *Lincoln*. You must love your country to name your son Lincoln."

The Germans move on. Jin looks up at Roosevelt. "Did you drlop-ew thse bomb on my countlry?"

"You mean Japan?" A stranger answers.

Jin remains quiet, didn't know he'd spoken aloud.

"Be careful who you blame. This is Teddy Roosevelt. You're thinking of Franklin, his fifth cousin, who was president during World War II. But even he wasn't responsible. He died before the war ended. Perhaps Truman, then, is the man for you to blame. But I don't, that decision may have saved my father's life. My father was a naval officer stationed in the South Pacific. And were there no bomb, perhaps my father would have been killed by your countrymen. Then who would stand here today to correct you?"

The stranger nods his head to himself. Not expecting a reply from Jin, he drifts off into the crowd.

Like strong liquor, the words of the stranger sink deep in Jinshirou. They evaporate blood, make a hole loneliness silently fills.

A Chinese man leans in toward the hollow Jinshirou, his voice is raspy, muted, controlled. "Blame? Are you still looking for someone to blame? How about your country? How about yourself? Perhaps your history classes forgot to mention that Japanese soldiers slaughtered three hundred thousand Chinese citizens in Nanking alone -- one by one -- before that war ended. Are you still so sure *blaming* is the answer?"

The hydrolic brakes of a tour bus release. Their wind-wisp sound mocks Jinshirou. It's a release of tension he yearns for, but cannot embrace.

Forty Japanese tourists armed with cameras and video shuffle from the bus, rush past Jinshirou to the Mountain. The group sparks in a clatter of snapshots, then, seemingly a moment later, stampede back to the bus. The door squeaks shut. Engine revs loud. They're gone.

Jinshirou stands in his hole of loneliness; the mountain of mammoth faces look down at him. Never had he heard of this mountain. Never had he thought Americans had a right to be proud. His parents had never spoken of Nanking. And even Aro believed Roosevelt was the American president at the time Nagasaki blew up. Jin begins to laugh to himself, at himself; laugh till he begins to cry. Dry cracking tear ducts in his eyes ache from years of dormancy. Inside, they pump like hydraulics. Outside, they flood his face with sorrow.

A little girl comes upon him. "Are you okay, Mister? Are you lost?" She points at the spot the tour bus had been. "Did they forget you?"

Jinshirou wipes his eyes with the backs of his hands. "I *was* lost." He smiles through smearing tears. "But-ew just now rlemembered my way."

"Really?" The girl's eyes brighten. "Good, then can you help me and my little sister? We're still lost."

Jin sees another little girl sitting on a park bench kicking her legs around, her eyes a bit watery.

Jinshirou wipes his runny nose. "Hai. Yes. Your mommy? She looks-ew like what?"

"She's kind of tall, she has green eyes, and these goofy old lady glasses. She has her hair up today, and, and her hair is like my hair, but darker. And um, she's got a red T-shirt on, that me and my sister bought her for Mother's Day last year, or maybe the year before. And you know what? My grandmother says she wears way too much make-up."

The two girls have taken Jin by each hand as the older talks. The three walk about the grounds seeking their mother.

"And your fathzer? He looks-ew like what?"

The girl responds matter of factly, "Don't know, I never met him." She turns to her little sister who is beginning to wail. "Hey um, Mister, Ruthie is crying. Can you put her up on your shoulders? That's what my mom does when she starts crying."

Careful to keep his hat on. Jin reluctantly lifts the girl up on his shoulders. It causes his wounds some pain. Ruthie stops crying, but her hands hold onto his face, bump his wound, smear his tears. One hand holding the hand of the older sister, the other holding Ruthie and the cap.

A middle-aged woman with too much make-up spots Ruthie floating above the crowd. "Ruthie!"

"Mommy!" Ruthie shouts back.

The older sister runs to Mom. Jin carefully lifts Ruthie off his shoulders, back to the ground.

Mom hugs both of her kids, rubs the sniffles from her nose. "Where did you two go? I swear I can't turn my head for one second! You two really scared me. You really scared me!" Shaking her head, balancing the so very recent fear of loss, with the more recent reunion, her confusion finally abates long enough to notice the teary-eyed Jin. "How can I thank you?"

"You just did."

"I mean, there are so many *weirdoes* out there. How can I thank you?"

Though she really means it, she doesn't expect an answer, her attention back to her newly found kids.

Jin watches the family reunite, longs for his mother's love. Under his breath, he answers her question to himself, "Forgib me."

Arlen's mother greets relatives next to the open casket. They hug her one by one.

"He was a good boy." Aunt Mary says.

"I know," Arlen's mother responds, "I know."

The major stands beside her silent, sad, strong for the family.

Jinshirou fastens a thin vine to a stick. Pulling a dead horse fly from his pocket, he ties the fly to the line, then wiggles it over the water. By twilight his forearm muscles are too tired to continue. He sighs, rips the vine from the stick, searches for a sharp-edged stone, then whittles one end of the stick to a point. Along the trunk of a very slanted tree, Jin walks out over the pond. Hugging the trunk he waits, then strikes a brown trout with his first spear thrust.

After cooking and eating that fish, Jin crawls out on the trunk again to wait for another, but falls fast asleep like some lazy panther. Across the pond, just a few steps from the quieting campfire, a bobcat's eyes reflect the light of the flames.

The morning crawls up his back. Warms his neck and head. Jin wakes to his own face reflecting in the pond below. Without breaking his own stare, he sharpens the stick further, cuts out Silitei's stitches one by one. They float down the stream like flies, trout nibble at them.

A man dressed as a Bobcat jumps into the air. The crowd shouts even louder. A group of guys gather around the TV set as the cheerleaders walk in front of the Mascot.

"Now that's what I'm talking about! Who needs the damn cat!"

"I'm telling you SDFU is gonna womp these guys."

"Shut up, you're an idiot."

"No, you shut up and get me a beer."

"You got a beer."

"Oh yeah."

"See, now who's the idiot?"

"Both of you shut up, I'm trying to watch this game."

Into the window of their Rapid City home, Jinshirou peers from an adjacent rooftop.

"You can watch while we talk, it's not like we're standing in front of you."

"Good thing, remember what happened last time."

"Oh yeah, no one wants to clean up another mac-cheese spill."

Jin watches for several minutes, then moves on. He climbs above the residential homes, peering in. "Amerlicans, who are you thzat Aro hate so much?"

In one house, a woman learns Mozart on the piano. In another, a man picks his nose with a cotton-tip. In the red brick one, a boy makes a tent out of blankets, reads comics with a flashlight. In a condo, two girls make brownies for their school fundraiser.

In an apartment building, a father puts his pre-teen daughter to bed. He kisses her head. "Now, you relax and have happy dreams." But the father's assurance doesn't seem to relax his daughter. He tucks her in, then kisses her on the lips. "Okay, honey, don't lock your door again tonight, or daddy will be real mad. Okay honey?"

Jin narrows his eyes, but cannot hear the whispers.

Through another window Jin watches two kids play video games. Through another, a group of teen girls giggle over a yearbook. Some rooftops later, Jin comes across a dark, rundown house. Pink streetlights beam through the window, catch one photo -- a black and white of the Hiroshima mushroom cloud. Jin scales along to get a better look. No cars in the garage.

He climbs through the attic window of the two-story frame house. Stepping up to the photo. "Why you decorlate wiss dis?"

Jin lights a candle, carries it from one photo to the next. All of bombings, one to the next, all are bombings. Near the TV lay two videotapes labeled OK City bombing and NY bombing. At the edge of the table, an answering machine. Jin taps the announcement button and lowers the volume: "Yeah, this is John. I'm off fishin' till Tuesday. Leave a message if you wanna."

The doorknob slowly turns. The door is not locked. The daughter pretends to be sleeping. The father is not deterred, he pets the girls head, pulls his trousers down and proceeds to kiss her. Her eyes close tight, tears squeeze forth.

"Dis is your daughter."

Father looks up in horror. Daughter keeps her eyes tightly shut. In the corner of her room, Jinshirou stands in makeshift Ninja clothing. Gathering pointless courage, father grabs the lamp off the nightstand swinging, still glowing. The light streaks, stains the man's vision, cord snaps dark. The effort completely desperate, completely inaccurate, Jin needn't dodge. The man falls to the floor tripping over his own trousers. Jin grasps him by the scruff of his neck, throws him against the dresser. A disk in the man's back slips. Father closes his eyes now tightly shut.

"She is your frlesh. Hab you no face?" Jin blows heated air from his nostrils. "Flrom tonight-ew I will lreturn. You cannot know when. I plromise your arlmighty God, if I find you in here pants down, I swear to your God, I will kick off your fuking nutz-ew."

Father opens his eyes in fear, but the room is empty, save for his whimpering daughter. The man falls to his knees crying, "I am so sorry, darling. I am so sorry."

David, Mr. & Mrs. Saoshita and Detective White sit in the gray Souix Falls police department.

White speaks, "I know this is hard. It's just hard. But, your boy needs help. Do you have any idea where he might have gone? An Uncle? A Friend?"

The parents' blank stares offer no answers. David scratches his head, then repeats the question as best as he can in inadequate Japanese.

Mrs. Saoshita, sad, despondent, remains quiet. David scratches his arm, taps his foot in discomfort. Mr. Saoshita responds briefly in Japanese.

"No, Detective White. They don't know." David finally finishes.

White leans back with a sigh that blends frustration and sympathy.

Rapid City, South Dakota, noontime business workers rush to and from lunch. Suits and hot dogs, skirts and sushi. The sun pounds straight down from the sky, the sweat drips from Jin's baseball cap as he strolls the boulevard. Taxis stop, accelerate off. Delivery boys weave aptly between cars and buses. The sidewalks bustle with focused citizens, laborers and shoppers. A drunkard urinates between two buildings. A young man offers watches for sale, pulls back his sleeve to show Jin a wrist full of watches. "Five bucks, any one of 'em."

"No sank you."

Jin crosses the street, waits for the light to change. Something catches his eye. A ski mask on the dashboard of an idling car. The bank clock toggles time and weather: 12:25 PM/ 95 degrees. Jin steps up to the corner to look a little closer. The driver taps fingers on the steering wheel, glances nervously across the street into the bank.

Shoppers Vivian Ollarglass and Ev Hansen converse at the stop light where Jin stands.

"And then Sarah told him, 'Well if you're gonna force me to teach 5th grade, well then, I'm just gonna have to accidentally mention a few bits of your unfortunate past...'"

Ev's eyes light up with interest in the gossip. "She said that to Bill's face?"

"Yep. Well, Bill started to act as if he had no idea of what Sarah was talking about. But she just kept going, 'like for instance the time you and Miss...' then Bill butts in and says..."

Ev interjects, "Okay already! You can teach your goddamn little second graders!"

"You bet that's what he said!" Vivian finishes.

The lights change, the two older women cross, Jin shuffles along behind them, one eye on the car with the ski mask.

Ev nods and starts her story, "Hey, did you hear about Ben?"

"Stetsons? The drunk?" Vivian is up for the latest.

"Yeah, well, I heard he walked right up to Pastor Dave and told him that he's an alcoholic and needs help."

"Wait? ... that Pastor Dave was a drunk?"

Ev chuckles, "No. No. That he, himself, Ben, was a drunk."

"No, really?"

"But, wait... now this is not substantiated, but as good a rumor as any, that he also confessed to abusing his daughter. Ben, not Pastor Dave."

Vivian's eyes droop. "Little Lynny? Oh my God."

"Yes. Can you believe that?"

"Oh my God, what did Dave say?"

The two chatting women enter the corner shoe store, Jin joins them, but sits in a chair that faces the window. He tries on a pair of tennis shoes while doing his best to both watch that car and listen to the two women gossip.

A third woman already in the store pops up as they walk in. "Ev? Viv? Did you hear?"

"Surprise, surprise, look who's here," Vivian whispers to Ev.

"Jane Whittlen," Ev whispers back, then louder to Jane, "Goodness, what?"

Jane's eyes beam with false modesty. "We won the lottery! The State lottery!"

"No kidding!?" Vivian pretends to care, "*You?*"

"Well, Don," Jane corrects, "but that means *me*, right?"

Ev shakes her head. "Geeze, that was fourteen thousand, wasn't it?"

"Twelve" Jane corrects again.

"But still -- twelve!"

"So do tell! What are you going to do with that money?"

"Well, I gotta go -- but I just bought a new pair of those K. Austins." Jane holds up a box of new shoes with pride, then leaves in a rush.

The driver, across from the bank, lights a cigarette with his nervous fingers. He puffs twice, puts it out almost as fast.

"Can you believe that? Twelve grand!" Ev looks at Vivian.

"You know what? ... Speaking of money..."

"Or lack there of."

"Speaking of money, I've gotta make a stop at the bank. Come on."

The two return to the streets without trying on a single pair of shoes. Jin places the tennis shoes back into the box, strolls behind.

"Anyway, what did Dave do?"

"Well, I don't know that either. But I'll bet beads to buckles, you'll see Ben Stetsons at your AA meeting tonight."

The conversation brings the two, and Jin, into the bank. Vivian opens her purse at the customer counter, pulls out a withdrawal slip.

"What's that supposed to mean? ... *'my meeting'*?"

"Well didn't you used to..."

"That was ages ago!"

"Anyway, the rumor thickens. Get this, a Kung Fu guy appeared in his house like a vision or something and told him to straighten up."

Jin pulls out a brochure on checking accounts, pretends to peruse. Instead, he's surprised to see a ski mask draping out of the pocket of a man near the door. The man also pretends to read a brochure.

"Whose house? Ben Stetsons's? This just gets better, doesn't it?

"A Kung fu guy? In South Dakota?"

The man yanks the mask from his pocket, pulls it over his face. Two other masked men also appear, lock the bank door from the inside. They draw the shutters, and their guns. "Okay, everybody hit the floor!"

Twenty-four people are in the bank lobby. All but the trio of armed men drop to the floor. Ev slides between Jin and a short stocky man. Her expression has become much more serious, somber, but her wits have placed her away from Vivian and near the two strongest looking fellows in the bank. Jin glances over to Ev, puts his finger to his lips, "Ssssh." Noticing a bulldog tattoo on the stocky fellow's arm, Jin whispers to him, "Malrines?"

Private Alvarez responds, "Yeah. What are you? A fuckin' Ninja?

Jinshirou smiles and shakes his head to himself. "Somesing like."

Ev's eyes widen.

Jin points with his eyes. "I take-ew two on thse lebt. Can you take-ew thse man who commands?"

Alvarez grimaces in skepticism, "If you can get the two... I sure as hell can get that one."

"No killing."

"Yeah, right. You just get your two."

"You hab-ew weapons?"

"Ankle knife."

"Show me."

Alvarez lifts his pant leg exposing the ankle holster and knife.

Shoji cries, "But Jinshirou will kill me."

"We must learn real knives. If your first encounter with a real knife is a worldly conflict, you will lose. You must gain confidence so that the sight of a knife will make you feel strong. Even if it is in the hand of your opponent." Aro has one hand on Shoji's head, one hand on Jin's. The boys are eleven and ten.

Shoji shakes his head. "He will kill me."

"He is your friend." Aro smiles, "Do you really think he will kill you?

Shoji turns his worried eyes toward Jin and nods a silent 'yes.'

Aro turns toward Jin too. "Jinshirou, would you kill your friend?"

"Not on purpose." A nervous Jin responds.

Shoji's eyes widen and water.

Aro chuckles, "Jin, is that all you are afraid of?"

"No," Jin looks at Shoji's feet. "What if he? I mean he's not..."

Shoji's blood begins to curdle as he anticipates what Jin is about to say.

"I mean," Jin continues, "he's not so good with implements, what if he accidentally kills me?"

Shoji lunges toward Jin in anger, the sharp edge of his small knife pointing. Jin blocks, the blade scrapes against his young forearm drawing blood. Shoji grabs for Jin's face with his free hand, Jin's block takes Shoji's knife full circle, breaking the surface skin of Shoji's shin and ankle. The pain is lost in anger.

Jin thrusts his forehead into Shoji's neck, Shoji backward tumbles to the temple ground. Before Shoji can even think to retaliate, Jin's short blade pinches Shoji's chest. Shoji drops his knife in defeat.

Aro laughs, he claps his hands, pulls Shoji up. "Congratulations boys. You are now men."

Alvarez's skepticism now turns to something much more grave. He looks Jin over, searching in his eyes, he decides this young punk Japanese fellow may actually be serious. Alvarez pulls the knife from its holster, hands it to Jinshirou. "I'm not sure why I should trust you... but I do."

The third robber places his gun on the counter to more quickly gather the cash.

On the floor behind a desk, Jin brings the knife up to his own eyes, the sharp reflection off the blade sets the wound in his upper arm singing a memory of pain. Then in a movement that catches Alvarez by surprise, Jin casts the blade across the room. Snapping the power cord, a lamp tilts to the floor, sparks. By the time Alvarez turns back to find him, Jin is fifteen feet away, two masked thieves under his knees. Ev gasps, Alvarez takes down the third man without a single shot fired. He laughs at the silly thieves, picks up the gun from the counter and points it at the masked man.

"Don't shoot!" A scared shaking voice comes from the mask. "Please don't kill me, man!"

Alvarez laughs, then whispers to the masked man, "Pow. Pow. Pow."

Bystanders laugh nervously along. Jinshirou looks at the carefree Marine with sadness for Arlen as he ties up the two bad guys with lamp cords. He gives their guns to the elderly security officer who had been cowering in the corner.

"I'm sorry." The security guard holds his head down in shame.

"Me, too." Jin pulls the knife from the wall. He reaches down to slide the knife back into the Marine's holster, while holding his hand on Alvarez's tattoo. "I am the one who is solry."

"What?" Alvarez puckers his face. "Did you scratch my blade, man?"

Jin stands and takes toward the door. "Somesing like."

"Hey! Where you goin'?" Alvarez looks up while keeping a good grip on the bad guy. "Hey, gimme a hand here. What'm I gonna tell the cops?"

"Tell thzem, I forlgot Nagasaki."

"...was one of the most devastating bombings of the decade. Of the four bombers we've researched in this video, only one was ever convicted. V. Douglas Starkler is currently at a Dallas prison, and up for parole in 2012. Thanks for watching."

Video tapes are scattered on the coffee table alongside a can of opened beer and a nearly completely eaten sandwich. In the kitchen, Jinshirou helps himself to an apple from a refrigerator desperately in need of cleaning. The tape in the VCR clicks off and rewinds. Channel Five news pops on in the middle of a story. Jin scans the bombing photographs that line the wall on the way back to the TV set. That photo of Hiroshima stops him. He's frozen.

"Here's another update on that bizarre South Dakota slaying... The story just gets stranger. The main suspect, Jinshirou Saoshita, a twenty-year-old Japanese man, is missing from Brookings and Sioux Falls, but may have been seen in the western part of the state. A woman claims that a Japanese man fitting the suspect's description returned her children to her in the Black Hills area. And the latest is that an attempted Rapid City bank robbery was foiled by an ex-Marine and an unidentified Asian whose actions lead police to believe is the SDFU slayer. We'll keep you updated as the information comes in."

Jinshirou clicks off the TV set. He presses the button on the answering machine again. "Yeah, this is John. I'm off fishin' till Tuesday. Leave a message if you wanna."

A tackle box reels Jin's attention. He opens it, fully stocked save for bait. He opens the closet just to his left, rubber fishing boots, three poles and a brand new reel. "I don't sink you are fishing."

Jin checks the calendar then begins to dig through drawers, records, photos. Among the many items, Jin finds a library copy blueprint of the Chicago Daley Center.

"Why do you hab dis picture, fisherman?"

He checks up at the clock and decides to take a break from his investigation. Climbs out of an attic window and begins his rounds.

The colored light from the big screen TV reflects off the painted faces of the SDFU fans relaxing into the couch and recliner. Jin peers in from the same window he'd peered in the night before. The TV announcers banter:

"It's a long pass, Chiles gets creamed, but Yokoyama grabs it. Oh yes! Yokoyama scrambles for a couple more yards, but is taken down by Sharring. An exceptional catch by David Yokoyama, a player we really haven't seen much of here at South Dakota Falls University."

"That's right. Yokoyama, a junior, seems to be playing with a fire we've not seen from him before."

"What with Wykowski on the injured list, he'll be fielding a lot more of Chiles' throws."

"That should keep him jumping."

"Come on, be good. Chiles' is the best SDFU has."

"Actually, Chiles, as well as the rest of the Wildcats, is playing extremely well."

"That's a bit surprising, considering the tragedy that shook up this whole campus, just four days ago."

"You know what? I think they're taking it out on Florida State!"

Jin smiles sadly, "So solry, David, so solry."

He steps off the shingles down to his next house.

Ben Stetsons puts Lynny to bed. "Lynny, I'm... I'm sorry."

Ben tucks her in, a knock startles him. He turns to look out the window, finds nothing but the blue apathetic moon. The knock comes again, he steps down the hall to the front door. Again the knock. He sighs. Readying to face the truth. Trembling, he turns the knob.

"Come on, Ben." Pastor Dave stands ready to go.

Ben's tremble creeps up to his smile. "Yeah, I'm ready. Thanks for coming to get me."

Mrs. Stetsons stares blankly at the TV. The grinding of her teeth drowns out its audio.

Jin sleeps, his body stretched out on a magnificent bear skin rug on the fisherman's floor. The sun catches his cheek, his eyes open to a stack of magazines and a family photo album on the floor under an end table. He rolls over, flips the album open. Picture after picture of fishing outings without any family or any fish. A cabin in the woods, some hunting rifles, a downed deer. A quad parked at the edge of the pond. Slanted across the pond, a severely bent tree.

"I know you tree."

Jin slams the album shut, grabs his shirt.

A bobcat hugs a high branch in the slanted tree. It looks down on Jinshirou who sleeps on the skewed trunk out over the pond. The porous bark presses an imprint of itself onto Jin's cheek. **Pop!** Jin's head cocks up like a bird. **Pop!** Jin climbs down, sets out in the direction of the sound. A thick forested area calms into a clearing of tall grass, scratches Jin's thighs. At the far end of the clearing, a cabin.

Just in front of the cabin, the fisherman rocks back and forth on an ammo crate. He's fiddling with a radio controller. Jin descends into a crawl. He swims through the tall grass like a crocodile, finds a back window to the cabin, hops through. Plastic margarine containers line the shelves. Several are on the table, some open, some not. Inside, powders, chemicals, not butter.

Outside the cabin, John the fisherman sets a butter container out in the distance. He hobbles back toward the cabin, returning to his ammo crate. He picks up the radio controller, spits out some tobacco and sends a signal. But his anticipations dash off, he taps the little box controller with a convenient beer can. Then presses the button again. Again nothing. He looks out into the distance at the butter container as he pries open the little box. Pulling the nine-volt battery from its prongs, he touches it to his tongue. Nothing.

"Fuckin' generic batteries!" John tosses the dead battery out into the forest, then stumbles into the cabin for a replacement. "Where the hell did I ... aww shit."

Jin jumps out the back window and runs directly toward the butter container that John had left in the clearing. While John fumbles around for a fresh battery, Jin removes the receive unit from John's target container, runs back to hide along the outside wall of the cabin.

John finds a new cell, steps outside. Just as swiftly Jin is inside. Seated on the crate, John snaps the new battery into the radio transmitter. Jin places the receive unit in one of a stack of butter containers on the wall. John snaps the little box back together. Jin pauses inside the cabin.

"Maybe I will not be so quick-ew dis time."

"But don't cry when you're not really hurt, that's what my dad says, that's just being a baby." The boy spanks his wound. "Five stitches, but look, it's all healed now."

The boy rolls back his sleeve as he turns to his father downstream; he hops through the water splashing it into a spray. White light refracts in the mist, splitting into waves of orange, yellow, green, blue, indigo and violet.

Jin pulls Aro's mom out of his pocket. The photo, wadded up by David, Jin un-crumples, sets on the table with care. Gently strokes the corners as if it were a precious infant.

"Forgib me Aro Momma."

John shakes the box, stands up off the crate, presses the button. To his surprise the cabin explodes behind him. Air blast from the window sends him six feet forward, face down, back aching. The cabin continues to explode one container after the next. John covers his head with both hands, face down in the dirt, he closes his eyes and waits. The explosions conclude, but John waits longer. He hasn't heard a thing save for a ringing since the first bang.

The flash of light reflects across their faces like a camera's flash. Or lightning. They blink, but do not move.

Soldiers scurry like pigeons from Jinshirou's inept reaches. They fly away from Aro. Forty-five degrees to the pavement, soldiers dive behind trees, cars, trucks. Jin closes his eyes. Aro's head strikes the tarmac like a match.

David, in full uniform, tilts his candle to light a candle in Ollie's hand. And Ollie passes the flame to the next player. Wax drips down to the field. The stadium seems draped with stringed decorative lights, a flickering rippling pond of orange and yellow. Wax beads like tears. A video image of Arlen waves on the screen in silence.

The Rapid City football fans watch the after-game memorial on their TV set. The somber mood uneasily welcomed, they turn away from the big screen and set up a table for a card game. Jin leans his forehead against their windowpane. If they thought to turn their attention outside, they would see him staring in at their TV, at all those candles, at David.

Ben stares helplessly at a mustard-colored suitcase in the hand of his teary-eyed wife. "My God, Ben, I knew you had a drinking problem. Jesus, everyone in Rapid City knows. But..." She lowers her voice, glances at Lynny's door, "Our Lynny? Did you really expect me to stay with you? Did you really think I could sleep with you again after you touched my daughter like that?"

Ben winces with guilt, but the pain of losing his family is heavier than his pride. "Angel, I gave myself up. I brought myself in. I'm different now."

She ignores him. She calls toward Lynny's door, "Lynny, come on, you're ready. I'll send Uncle Mike to get... *whatever*, whatever you've forgotten to bring."

Lynny steps out of her room, her eyes to the ground. She's standing up, but so focused on the rug that she imagines her eyes two marbles rolling on the floor. A small backpack stuffed with things on her back, a fuzzy white bear in her hand. Mrs. Stetsons grabs Lynny's free hand and opens the door. Ben cries inside, dumbfounded outside. His wife stops to look Ben in the eyes one last time. "A long time ago, I thought you were really something..." anger bubbles in her trembling body. "How could you do this!"

"I, I didn't actually... you know," Ben looks down in helpless shame. "Go all the way."

His wife shakes her head, the eyes rush with water, but she slams the door before they fall.

Jin, at the window, looks down in a helpless shame that echoes Ben's. Hates himself for understanding disgrace more than the joy of children splashing in a river.

Rhonnie returns to her dorm room after the memorial event. Her candle barely an inch long by now, still hosts a flame. The wax has built up on her thumb and forefinger. She sits silently on her bed, slides the rose that Jin gave her from its place on her shelf. Expressionless, she brings the flame to the petals. Dry they snap, ignite, dissolve immediately into a hot amber ember. Carbon ashes drift slowly to her lap.

Jin glides between rooftops with grace, but without passion. His head down, disinterested in the many Rapid City residents, he heads back to his temporary residence, his squatting home. A candlelight's glow from a window across the alley catches his dragging eyes. He crosses the back street, then scales a tree near that window and peers in. The room is very neatly kept. A bookshelf, arm's length from the bed, hosts a collection of titles: *Do-it-yourself Home Improvement, Plato and the Greeks, Mozart in Austria, Japanese Made Easy.*

A woman sleeps with an eye mask covering half of her face. An open romance novel teeters at the edge of the bed. Jin moves from the tree to get a closer look. Leaning in now, both hands on the windowsill, Jin studies her nose and mouth. Not American. Asian for sure, maybe Japanese. Jin smiles at the gentle beauty between her upper lip and soft button nose.

"Why do you rlearn Japanese-ew?" Jin whispers to himself.

A rubbing sound disturbs his thoughts. He thinks to leave, then notices her hand gently stroking her chest under the sheets. Her lips gently part. She breathes softly, but rapidly. Jin's attention is focused on her lower lip, he becomes oblivious to all else. Pulpy maroon, but the candle's salmon glow swims across as her lips part, touch, part. An inchworm on a crisp green twig, Jin swings one foot inside the window. Then the other. Slower than a dream, softer than a flake of snow.

Jin has been trained in stealth. In a dim room, you cannot see him, cannot hear him. But now, less than three feet from the sleeping woman, his body heat escapes his quest for secrecy.

In her own fantasy world, in her own dream, the woman murmurs something in broken Japanese. It's soft and so broken that even Jin cannot piece it together. He lowers his ear just above her mouth, and to his surprise, she repeats just as faintly, but in English, "Kiss me."

Jin sharply turns his face toward hers as if to check that her expression is consistent with the words. Can she see him through her blinders? Has his body heat given him away?

"Kiss me," she continues, her lips abutting at the "m" then parting again.

Jin's face, just inches from hers, he does not move. The candlelight casts warm shadows like moon-filled clouds. Her soft words, her hand on her chest, those maroon lips.

"Okay, honey don't lock your door again tonight, or daddy will be real mad. Okay honey?"

Jin freezes. He closes his eyes in disgust at the father, at himself. But he is frozen. Bent over her face. Like a startled monkey, he clenches his eyes tighter in hopes that he will disappear. Become an illusion. Become a dream. Her dream.

"You're a killer, a murderer. I don't know you." Rhonnie's face still buried in her hands. *"I thought, I thought I loved you."*

Remnants of a dream, a near dream, the beginnings of a dream, torment him.

His eyes are locked tight, ashamed. As hard as he wishes it so, he is not a dream, nor has he disappeared. Still he is stealth, standing over the sleeping woman. His moist breaths leave his nostrils, fall upon her cheek, nose. She inhales sharply. Her chin ascends gently, as if levitated by a magician, as a balloon inflating. One inch, half an inch, her lips just one layer of skin away from his.

Jin's eyes break open, bloom in an instant. Every other muscle in his body remains locked.

Their lips touch the same slice of air, almost a membrane of air, the moisture almost completing the kiss.

Suddenly, she pulls her chin away, the back of her head drops to the pillow. She gasps in bewilderment, her lips now separate in half alarm. She sits up abruptly, ripping the sleep mask from her face, revealing eyes of worry, wonder, quiet, loneliness. She looks around the room a second, a third time, but there are only her walls to find. She stands, steps to the open window, the breeze drapes the light through her gown. She does not remember leaving it open. She pulls it shut. Locks. She sits back to the bed, the novel drops to the floor. She picks it up and grins to herself. A dream.

.

Knock, Knock.

Ben gets up to answer the door.

"Detective Brian White, Sioux Falls Police." White's voice vibrates through the old wooden door. He holds his badge up to the peephole.

"Jesus, I didn't go all the way! I can't believe they called you. They swore they wouldn't. They said I could trust them."

"Christ! I'm not here for you."

"What?" Ben readies himself to let it all go to hell. "Why not?"

"Mr. Stetsons, just open the door. I'm not here for you. I just need some information."

"What?"

"The word is that you had a visit by *some kung fu guy*. Could you tell me about it?"

Ben opens the door, T-shirt and pajama bottoms. "He ah, he saved my life. Saved my daughter's life."

White has no time for the irrelevant. "He's wanted for murder in Sioux Falls. Maybe you could focus on that for a second. Killed somebody's son. Sliced him up like a piece of bloody meat. I'm happy for you and your daughter, but I'm not here for that. You gonna help me find this guy or what?"

"Look, I don't know about the, the... killing. I couldn't help you if I wanted to. I don't know anything about him, only that he stopped me. He stepped in and saved my daughter from me."

White peers around the apartment. "Yeah, right, maybe he dropped his halo around here someplace."

PFFOW, PFFOW.

Richard, Tad, Denzel, Jimmy, replete in full military uniform, aim their rifles toward the sun rising in the East and shoot another round for Arlen six feet under. New soil covers his casket. Mrs. Williams, the Major, hold each other tightly. David, Ollie, Rhonnie watch in the distance. A crowd of close friends and caring SDFU students and faculty circle the plot.

PFFOW, PFFOW.

The crack of dawn fires through the bedroom window. Her hand drops off the edge of the bed. It wakens Jin sleeping underneath. But she dreams, soft blue mask eclipsing light. Bed springs above, her silky fingers dangle. He slides himself from under the bed, slips to the hallway, through a window into a leafy tree. Like a lizard, he stops, blends. Down across the street, Detective White is waiting out front of a home. A young Hispanic man leaves the house in work clothes, lunch box under his arm.

"Excuse me, I'm Detective White, Sioux Falls PD." White flips the badge, approaches Alvarez. "Sorry to bother you so early in your morning."

"Sure, is this about the bank thing the other day?"

White pulls a small book of notes from his back pocket. "You told Rapid City Police that a tall oriental man assisted you in foiling that robbery..."

Alvarez, jams a stick of gum between his smiling teeth. "That's right. This guy was unbelievable." His good mood contrasts White's lack of one.

"Yeah," White grunts, holds out a picture. "Is this him?"

Alvarez's cheeriness wanes with the weight of White's no-nonsense demeanor. "Yeah, I mean, I think so. I kinda had a few other things vying for my attention." He spits his gum back out onto the wrapper. "What? Is this guy wanted in Sioux Falls, or something?"

"You also told police that this man said, and I quote you, 'Tell them I forgot Nagasaki.'"

"Yeah, that's what he said." Alvarez pauses in an uncomfortable seriousness, "Hey, didn't we blow up that place in WWII?"

"That's right."

"I mean, like, nuked it to pieces?"

White looks away from Alvarez's piercing questions, almost a sigh of conscience, "Yeah."

"You don't happen to know the civilian casualties do you? I mean, how many people do you think got blown to dust?"

Detective White, not used to being interrogated, scratches his ribs, tilts his head, pushes his lips together, then apart. "Look, I don't care that we blew up some Japanese village 50 years ago. I don't care that this guy starts going around doing *'good deeds.'* The fact is he cut open the belly of an American citizen six days ago, here in South Dakota." White rolls up his sleeve revealing a bulldog tattoo, leans in heavily to Alvarez, his steely eye breaking hard. "Not just any American, a rookie Marine."

Mere moments earlier, Alvarez had hopped out of bed, showered, shaved, made his lunch whistling. He felt better than he'd felt in years and now all of that cheerfulness seems to be held at gun point. "I believe I've told you all I know. I think that's the guy in the photo. That's all I can say... *sir*." He finishes with military inflection.

BRRRING, BRRRING

An alarm clock sounds. The two men in the street look toward the house of the sleeping woman. Jin closes his eyes in the tree as not to be seen. Alvarez notices him immediately, but says nothing. White follows the line of Alvarez's sight, climbs it like a Marine shimmies along a rope. Jin darts off across the neighboring rooftops. White draws his gun and runs after, hopping fences, traversing yards, alleys.

She wakes, pulls the mask from her face, quiets the alarm clock, opens the window, looks out to the now empty street. She rubs her eyes, lightly touches her finger to her lip.

Jin up high, White on the ground. White dashes through one yard after another. Some blocks later, standing in a grassy yard, he runs out of steam, puts his hands on his knees to catch his breath, looks up in the trees.

"Toss the gun," A rough country voice baritones, "mother fucker."

White turns one-eighty toward the back end of a gray-sided home. A large figure sits on a tattered recliner chair on the back porch. The figure points a shot gun in White's direction.

White attempts to calm the man. "I'm a..."

"Shut the fuck up and toss the gun."

Fumes from his nostrils, White throws the gun to the side. It falls near a fresh pile of dog shit.

Josh disengages the rifle, relaxes, chuckles, spits out some chew, shouts, "All yours, Jobert!"

A large pit bull takes off from the porch with fierce speed and big teeth.

"Shit!" White lunges for the fence, but he's not young enough, not fast enough. The dog leaps to take a chunk out of his kidneys. Jin swings down from the trees, deflects the dog's jump with his body, both the dog and Jin slide into the bushes. Just as loud and quick as Jobert's sprint, now a quick quiet silence.

Josh's eyes narrow. "Jobert!" He stumbles to his feet, his great mass making the effort almost impossible. He lifts the rifle and squints down the barrel at White. White freezes at the fence.

Jinshirou emerges from the bushes. He's got the dog in a strong hold. Jobert whimpers, struggles to get free. In Jin's other hand, White's gun cocked and pointed at the dog's head.

Josh almost breaks to tears. "Oh my god. Don't shoot him. Don't shoot him."

"You don't shoot man. I don't shoot dog."

Josh stumbles back, nods head, drops rifle.

Jin approaches White who is now quite wet with sweat and fear.

"Lay on thse ground, Detectib White."

White lowers to one knee, then lays out on the ground. Jin aims the gun at White's head, laughs like Alvarez at the bank. "Pow. Pow. Pow."

Josh sparks into laughter too. Jin walks over to the porch. Hands Jobert to Josh's welcoming arms. He puts White's gun on the porch nearby. "He is police-ew. Do not shoot him."

Jin leaves. White slowly gathers his breath, stands, calmly, carefully walks up to the porch. "Could I? Wouldya?" White shakes his head, "Ahh hell! Give me my damn pistol back!"

Josh falls with all his weight back into the recliner, the pit bull on his lap, shot gun in one hand, White's gun in the other. "I don't know, I kinda like this one. It's shiny."

The Major's gun shines in the gleaming apathetic light of morning. Its steel chills his forehead, left temple, but it feels good, cooling, inviting. Every medal on his uniform buffed and gleaming, the Major sits calmly in his favorite chair, remembering. A parade of military photographs marches across his walls. Friends, buddies, some alive, some dead. Arlen, matted and framed, at the right. He pauses on Arlen, introspective, patient. He lowers the weapon, holsters it. Pats it twice.

A red flannel shirt overflowing barrel-chested overalls, Bret nibbles on a stem of hay as he loads a couple of fat pigs up on a flatbed Ford. The pigs are in no hurry, but not terribly opposed to Bret's directions either. He locks the gate on the truck. Drops into the driver's seat himself. The Ford sways with his weight, despite two pigs aboard. He fires up the engine, spins the wheels, but they only sink into the mud below. He pauses, gently presses the accelerator, sinks some more. Bret shakes his head at himself in the rearview, drops his forehead down on the steering wheel in frustration.

A crackle of stones startles him. Bret squints in the side mirror, an Asain man drops a second bucket of rocks in the mud around the left rear wheel.

"Tlry again."

Bret accelerates. Jin, back up against the truck, pushes the heavy four wheeler out of the rut.

Bret sticks his head out the window. "Hey, thanks!"

Jin brushes off muddy hands on dirty pants. "Which-ew way do you go now?"

"Chamberlain."

"Camper Land?"

"You ain't from 'round... ain't ya?"

Jinshirou's head rocks side to side in agreement. "No, I am not."

"'Tween here and Sioux Falls, 'bout half way 'tween."

"May I accompany you?"

"Ahhh, okay. I mean, no probum. Get in."

Jin climbs in.

"Don't know why you want to go there. It's just a borin' place. Ain't nothin' there worth spittin' at. 'Cept the slaughterhouse. Time to bring these fat ones up at choppin'."

Jin nods, exhausted from the morning chase, the walk out of town, and moving a 2-ton pick-up with two pigs and Bret.

"That's Bell and Piza. My auntie named Piza, said there's some town in Italia with a tower leanin' over, that it was built that way. Bell's a perfect pig, but Piza, she's born with her front leg a little short, she leans a bit. So Auntie named her Piza."

Jin's eyelids lower like blankets. Asleep beside him, Bret doesn't seem to notice nor mind.

"Don't matter though, they're up for slaughter... Bell and Piza are. Nothin' much up in Chamberlain. Can't believe you never heard of it, though."

Jin's sleep is intermittent.

"Well there's one other thing in Chamberlain... the boss' daughter..." Bret's eyes gloss over, he drives autopilot, examines his memory. "The sweetest lips. I mean some cranberry red lips, and blonde hair, too... strawberry blonde."

The sleeping woman's lips part.

"Old Jed's daughter, Maggie... she's somethin'. Just bout the perttiest girl in the state. That's what I think anyways. I mean, I don't know if she ain't got no boyfriend. I don't know, but her fingers, she's ain't got no rings..."

Her fingers slide from the roof of the pick up, pass through Jin's hair, caress his wound.

"Yeah, Maggie, wow, you know, I get such a feelin' in my gut when I see her. I can't even stand it. I really can't stand it."

The sleeping woman slides completely in through the window of the Ford. Like a kitten, she cuddles her head on Jin's chest.

Jin's eyes open for a second or two every five minutes; each time Bret is still running his mouth about Maggie.

"It's like I can barely open my mouth. I just can't find a damn thing. I think about her the whole ride up, every time, but then I get there, not a damn thing outta my mouth. That ever happen to you?"

For the first time in almost a full hour, Bret waits for a response from Jin, invites him into conversation. Jin is half-awake, half-asleep, enjoying the rest.

"Huh, Buddy?" Bret gives Jin a farmland shove on the shoulder.

Jin's eyes open in slight annoyance. Disappointed that his fantasies are only dreams, he remembers he's in the truck, pulls his hand from his pocket, Rhonnie's rain check.

"Didn't ya never feel like that?"

Jin needn't have been awake, nor understood English completely to get Bret's long-winded picture. Jin sighs in a breath of wakefulness, "Did you invite to her?"

"Whatya mean?"

"Asking her out? To dinner?"

"Ask her out? No way. I mean, no way. She's way outta my league. You ain't from 'round. You don't know how it works. I'm a pig rancher's son. The lowest of the low. *Only thing lower is the pigs.* "

Already bothered by the shove into consciousness, Bret's lack of any self-confidence hits Jin harder, knocks him out the door -- *literally*. Finding the latch, Jin opens the passenger door. At sixty mph, Jin slinks out, climbs in the bed of the truck to sit with the Bell and Piza.

Wind plows through the crack in his window. Used to not being answered, Bret doesn't notice that Jin no longer sits in the cab, resumes his monologue, "I mean, you dream about it. You dream 'bout askin' her out, but she's way outta your league -- just too beautiful. You can't ask. You'll just be crushed in the... in the... you know, the..."

Finally, Bret glances over to the empty seat. He gasps, checks the rearview, finds Jin fast asleep in the hay with the pigs. Bret's gaping mouth finally shuts. He realizes how dry his lips are, clicks open a can of lemonade and remains quiet at the wheel for the rest of the ride.

Jin thrusts his forehead into Shoji's neck, Shoji backward tumbles to the temple ground. Before he can even think to retaliate, Jin's short blade pinches his chest. Shoji drops his knife in defeat.

Aro laughs, he claps his hands. "Congratulations boys. You are now men."

Aro pulls Shoji up from the ground. "You lost because you knew you would lose."

"But Jin is better than me." Shoji rebuts.

"He is better because you believe he is."

"But I *am* better." Jin interjects.

"Did you hear that Shoji? Confidence is sharper than any knife."

Detective White sits at the kitchen table with a single mother sporting too much make-up. Ruthie and her big sister play in the next room. Ms. Dannals pours White a cup of hot coffee, takes a peek at her daughters nervously. "So... do you think he... ah..." She stops pouring to hold back a few tears.

"Abused them?" White surprises even himself with frankness. The thought had not occurred to him until just now.

The worried mother's eyes are all tears now as she nods, preparing herself for the worst news.

White scratches his head at the possibility. "No." White reflects, "You know what? I don't think so."

"How can you be sure? I mean, how can you be sure?"

"I think he got what he wanted." White bites his lower lip. "He was looking for revenge and he got it. A pay back. Your daughters, they had nothing to do with any of that."

"But that COIT boy, did he? What did he have to do with it?"

Bret pulls to the shoulder of the exit ramp to Chamberlain. He hobbles around back to the pigs and wakes Jinshirou. "Why'd you do that? Why'd you go back here?"

Twice awakened by Bret, and this time to the harsh smell of farm animals, Jin's patience wanes. "You are pathetic... *pathetic*, and you lie."

Bret's hard round head tilts like a dog unsure of a loud command. He takes one step back with Jin's words. "Well that's a bit mean. I mean, pathetic maybe, but not a liar."

"You say these pigs-ew are lower thzan you. So you lie, you are thse lower one. You are lower thzan pigs-ew! See thzem... content as birds in tlrees. You are lower thzan thzem. Thzat makes-ew you a liar."

Bret retorts defensively, "They're goin' to choppin'. If they're so damn cool it just shows how stupid they are!"

"Thzey are go to slaughter. But thzey still love demselves. Today thzey die, but you are alleady dead. You slaughter yourselb eberlyday. Eberly night you spend alone, you sharpen thse knibe."

Bret's eyes fill with tears and anger. Rather than actually hearing the words of this foreigner, Bret lets his blood curdle. His fingers curl up into fists, his forearms tense.

"Eben now, you stand a coward. I insurlt you. I sleep wiss your pigs-ew, just to get away flrom you. Hab you no face?"

Veins begin to pulse in Bret's temples, his neck begins to vibrate with anger, frustration. He locks tight in indecision, inaction. He is a fireplug ready to burst, but does nothing, chokes.

Jin slides to the tailgate, dangles his legs down, picks up some pig shit and tosses it at Bret's feet. "Maggie rathzer dance wiss Piza thzan you."

Bret's internal fireman cranks the wrench with both hands, the cap pops, water sprays upward as Bret lunges forth. His large mass propels Jin back into the flatbed. A walrus atop a shark. Bret grabs Jin's head with both hands and shoves it back into a fresh pile of Piza's newest creation. Bret's face is red with anger, humiliation and tears.

Shit caking off his head, Jin begins laughing. It's a deep laughter, a laughter lost inside him since childhood.

Bret backs off, confused, dumbfounded, quiet.

Jin's laughter finally subsides, smile remains. "I knew you still hab some face!"

Bret's bloodshot eyes slowly soften, his pounding breath slowly calms. He stares at Jin for a long time. "Man, *who are you?*"

In a cheap hotel, Detective White pages through the Rapid City phone book. His open suitcase on one side of the bed, he sits on the other with the phone between his chin and shoulder. "I don't know. This guy, he's getting under my skin. He's not your normal psycho."

Captain Lou Branchette's voice pierces his ear, "*Normal psycho?*"

"Yeah, that's funny. It's like in Sioux, he set the town on fire. But here... " He pauses to recollect Jin body slamming the charging pit bull. "here, they, they think he's a god-damn angel."

"*Normal psycho? God-damn angel?* ... Angel's don't cut up innocent people. Christ, Brian, weren't *you* a Marine?"

White looks himself in the mirror. "Look Lou, I'm gonna check out a few more things here tonight. I'll be back in the office tomorrow."

"Brian, he's a murderer. Forget everything else, even if only because it's the law. Just bring him in."

The freight train creaks and squeals along the tracks, it's been slowing for thirty minutes, now down to a crawl. Jin's crooked hairline looks out the rusty door as the train nears the Falls area. The trees seem so much greener than he remembers, have they had rain? On the side of the tracks, steel piping has replaced the vine-bound cable. Crossing gates lower in anticipation of the train. Jin leaps to the ground before the intersection. He dashes into the woods and up a tree.

Below and to the right, the lovers have returned to their spot, they entangle in the back seat of a shiny sports car. "**Make Love Not War**," the bumper sticker reads.

About twenty-five feet from the car, in the bushes, a teen. Between the teen and love scene an SLR camera, a tripod and a long telephoto lens. This teen is familiar, Dan, the one that suggested cutting the train cable.

A bobcat darts out in front of the car, the male lover looks up. Though his face is not known to Jin, all of America knows this actor.

"What is it?" Asks his lover.

"Wow, a big cat, a bobcat or something. Didn't you see it? It was pretty awesome."

She smiles. The movie star notices a glimmer in the bush and squints. The sun's light gleams off the camera lens. Dan freezes, busted. He grabs the tripod, camera, and scurries off.

"Shit," the actor pounds the seat. "It's another fuckin' reporter. I'm sorry, Brenda, I thought we'd escape that shit out here.

"I don't need these kind of problems." Brenda drops her head.

The teen blasts off on a dirt bike.

Detective White sits at a library table amidst scattered books on WWII, the Hiroshima and Nagasaki bombings in particular. He pages through photos while listening to audiotapes, one from a reporter on an observation plane:

"...But the cloud is not just huge, it is a living totem pole, carved with many grotesque faces grimacing at the Earth."

A small red light in a dark room burns the color of the devil unto Dan. He grimaces. Photos of the naked celebrity and lover are strewn across a wire, held by paperclips as they drip. Dan rinses another red-hot sexy image in the sink with one hand, reaches with the other into his pants, zipper open like a book.

Dan whispers to himself, "Duuuuuude! I'm gonna make a mint with this one!"

A blinding flash breaks across the room, the light reaches every dark corner, like a spark in a grain mill.

Shocked, Dan rips his hand from his pants as if to start a lawn mower. "Who's there?"

"You will make a mess wiss thzat one."

"Who the fuck is that? I'll kill you."

"If onlry you can." Jin states blankly.

Dan zips up his pants, fumbles for a flashlight, shines Jin from the shadows. Jin allows the light. Seeing Jin's size, Dan decides talk might be a better option. "Look, I took the photo. They were in a public area. It was totally legal."

"Is your heart not disturlbed thzat you ruin a people's libes?"

Dan narrows his eyes. "I know you. You're that jap that killed the COIT guy at SD. Duuude, and *you're* lecturing *me* on ruining lives?"

Jinshirou sombers. His face becomes like stone, lit in the dark by a 3-volt bulb, he's a sullen ghost. "Do you know anothzer more quarlified?"

Selfishly resilient. "It's my picture. I took it legally and there is no fucking way I'm not collecting."

Click

Jin flips the wall switch, two six-foot fluorescent tubes dizzy with energy, they sputter into whiteness and illuminate the room. Dan quickly covers a roll of undeveloped film with a towel. But pauses just as fast seeing his camera in Jin's hand.

"And dis is my picture. I do not care if it is rlegal to take. But if you sell yours, I sell mine."

"Hey, that's not fair!"

"What is your picture's title? I title dis one 'hands in pants.'"

Still staring at the photo of Hiroshima now in his hands, White stands and walks to the librarian on duty. "Ah, ahm, ah, you don't happen to have any of those old movies... *Tora Tora Tora*, and ... I don't know, those old black and whites about WWII, Pearl Harbor, Hiroshima, all that?"

The librarian doesn't answer right away. She waits for White to look her in the face, her Japanese face. "May I ask why you are so interested in Hiroshima?"

White backpedals in embarrassment. "I'm. I didn't ah, I didn't mean anything by it."

"I didn't take anything by it." She responds without accent, "I'm interested in Japan myself. Anyway, you can find those in the history section of the videos rack," she points, "which is just over there."

Unsure how to respond, White decides to bow as he backs away to the rack. She bows back, then softly chuckles to herself.

Jin climbs the last few cast iron rungs on the fire escape. One leg over the rooftop ledge, he smiles at Silitei. Silitei sits on his box, roasting some meat high above the city. "You know, you left before teaching me to catch pigeons," Silitei flips the small piece of beef, "but I bet a dove's capture is easy after killing a child."

Jin stops in his track, his head drops as if guillotined.

"You're quite famous, yellow man. I am also surprised to see your face again." Silitei has no good cheer. This time the gruff is not for show, it comes from the bone. "When you stopped his heart -- you stopped our hearts. You dropped a bomb on Sioux Falls, and now we're dying slow painful deaths."

Jinshirou's eyes bleed tears. "Sank you..." he steps back down the cold black ladder, "... for attending my wounds."

Standing in front of Arlen's photo, as if for days, the Major pets his oblivious, purring cat.

. Flickering images of airplanes gunning down soldiers as they storm a cold gritty beach soar across Detective White's face in the A/V room of the Rapid City library.

Jin drops a dozen roses on the front steps of his parent's temporary home. He peeks in, a strange white face peeks out at him. A man in a **car parked** across the street spills coffee on himself while reaching for the door handle. Jin is gone before the car door opens.

Det. White hunches over the library table, his chin against an article about Einstein and the A-bomb. A woman approaches.

"Detective White?"

"Oh!" Startled, White throws his eyes open like a freshman in History 101. "Mrs. Williams. My God. You scared the..." He calms. "Jeez, what are you doing here?"

"Looking for you."

"How'd you know I was here?"

"Apparently, you're easier to find than our Ninja."

White rolls his eyes to the side in mild embarrassment. "So... please sit down. What ah, what can I do for you?"

Mrs. Williams sits slowly onto the library chair. Her movement is eerie, almost ghostly. Her flesh and muscles seem so wrought, wrung like wet laundry, wrought of any care for herself. Colorless, meatless, her skin and organs rest like tofu on her fragile bones. Those bones bump against the hard wood chair and rest. Her eyes emptied of even their last tears are now dried open. They roll over the books strewn in front of Det. White. The bombs in Japan, images of charred and dismembered Japanese citizens slip in through her pupils. They rest on her retinas just as her bones hold her tofu flesh. "I want to know why my son was killed."

White wipes his brow nervously, scratches the stubble on his cheek, sighs, "*Our Ninja*, Jinshirou Saoshita, was the choice student of Aro Tomako. Aro's family was wiped out when the US dropped an A-bomb on Nagasaki.

"I thought it was *Hiroshima*?"

White pages through one of the books. "Yeah, look, it was. That was August 6th, 1945. Nagasaki was August 9th."

A tremble reaches Mrs. Williams's otherwise impossibly peaceful voice, "Two bombs?"

"Well, I've just been going over all of this recently too. I mean, relearning the history. We, the US, we were creamin' them -- dropping conventional bombs on all of their cities..."

Mrs. Williams' eyes still have not blinked, but now they gloss as she visualizes her father, the Major, standing at the wall of war pictures, holding the family cat.

White continues, "...We were sending air raid after air raid. But they just would not give up..."

White's narrative ignites old memories, war stories told by the Major. Though he'd refrained from talking about the battles for decades, Mrs. Williams recalls the tales in the visual: **The Major steers his plane "The Bobcat" through a sky full of planes and parachuting pilots. The bullets** spray from his guns on each side like train tracks. Zeros explode, Japanese parachuters pop like water balloons. Their blood rains from the sky.

"... The casualties on both sides were very very high... Truman decided to try out the A-bomb as a way of forcing the Japanese to surrender. The thing was huge. It was devastating. I mean it wiped out, like, 30,000 people -- *like that*. The city was pretty much blown off the map..."

The librarian looks up from her computer screen at White and Mrs. Williams, a bluish glow on her narrow glasses.

Mrs. Williams lets go of her memories. "So why the second bomb?"

"The US waited for the Japanese response, but well, some of these books say that the Japanese government... things were just so chaotic... it was war time, the country was in shambles... they just didn't get it. They just didn't know the destructive power of the bomb. I mean, the US warned them. They dropped pamphlets in the streets, warning the people of this big bomb."

"So because the US could only wait three days before they killed another 30,000 people, my son is dead?"

"It was wartime Mrs. Williams. People's sons were dying everyday..."

BRAZZZZZZ.

Suddenly, an alarm pierces their ears. White gasps, but Williams' body has no longer the ability to be shocked. Finally, the clanging terminates, echoes.

A second later, a gentle voice amplified, "I'm sorry about that annoyance." The librarian explains, "The fire alarm was needlessly pulled. There's nothing to worry about, it's not a real fire... And we've caught the prankster... Mrs. Albertsen, would you please come to the reference desk and claim your son."

After spending a few seconds trying to get a glimpse of the prankster, White turns back to Mrs. Williams hoping that she'll be relieved after the false alarm. She has not changed her expression.

Veronica McKale swims to the surface, breaststrokes, then down, then up. She reaches the edge of the pool and pauses for a breath. A hand runs through her tangled wet red hair. She knows that touch even without turning her eyes, which quickly fill with chlorine and rage. "You've got some fucking nerve, coming back here!"

"But... " Jin kneels, "You don't... I..."

"I swear to God, if you don't leave *now,* I'll scream."

Jin stands, serious and sad. He looks around nervously, then steps away.

"You *fucking* bastard! I don't even know you!"

A sharp blade cuts into Piza's neck. The blood flows from her artery like pool water. Legs tied, flat on her side, Bret witnesses the life leave her body. No longer fit to be called **pig**, Piza's carcass is now pork.

Bret slaps himself in the face. The smack echoes in the back of the cold blue slaughterhouse; even Piza's butcher turns his head to see its source. But Bret has already charged out to the offices. Without a word of explanation, he approaches Maggie. Maggie glances up from her invoices, points at the phone against her ear. It's nearly five and she's trying to finish up.

Uncharacteristically impatient, Bret blurts, "Maggie?"

Maggie nods, clicks off the phone, her nose in the forms, pen scribbling. "Yeah, hold on Bret, I'm almost finished here."

"Come to dinner with me."

Maggie looks up with surprise. "Uhm, well I, I made arrangements with my sister and her husband." She takes a breath and turns back to the deskwork.

Bell's groans faintly rumble behind closed doors. Bret can smell Bell's life force spread away from her body as the blood flows across the concrete butchering station.

"Break them."

"I'm sorry," Maggie tosses the last invoices into a file, "*what?*"

"Come on, Maggie, just join me for dinner."

"Sure, Bret," Maggie reminds, "but I told you, I made arrangements with my sister."

Already far into uncharted territory, Bret begins to realize his stomach is floating off, his eyes begin to blink twice at a time, air pressure pushes his temples inward. The comfortable idea of retreat paints across the inside of his mind. He relaxes in it. He nods in agreement, he jams his hands in his pockets and, just as he turns to leave Maggie, the memory of Jin sleeping with his pigs drops into his head.

Piza's skull cracks and is removed from her body.

Bret stops even before the turn. "Your sister lives here, I only come but when the pigs need..." Bret presses his lips one to the other. "Just call her and cancel. Is it really such a big deal?"

Maggie smiles, squints her eyes at Bret. The smile radiates quietly until she picks up the phone, speed-dials. "Yeah, Jamie, Maggie. Yeah. Yeah. Something came up, can we do it next week? Great. See ya then."

Bret smiles even bigger, his forehead grows with floating eyebrows.

"Whoa, Bret Olson!" Maggie grabs her nose. "Yer takin' a shower before yer takin' me anywhere!"

Jinshirou stands alone amidst the rows upon rows of white round-topped tombstones. They grow from the ground like teeth, biting in anger at the sky. But the jaw is locked in six feet of dirt. But the real fury has long been drained from once pumping arteries. Or passed on to those whose blood still circulates. Passed on so that more teeth will grow from green pastures.

Japanese tradition, Jinshirou kneels, lays food, a hamburger, at the grave of Arlen J. Williams. He lights a dozen sticks of incense, pokes them in the dirt. Jin steals the air, his lungs grow with the sudden surge. Though the incense stings his sinuses, he breathes hard again. Then stands.

Apparently apathetic clouds, white like stones, float across the transparent sky. The sun moves at its usual pace, tracking Jin's shadow from one stone to the next. He can find no reason to leave this place.

Photo of Arlen released from the wall, but firmly captive in his trembling hands, the Major stumbles from his car. Eyes fixed on the photo, the Major can see nothing else. He drops to his knees at Arlen's grave. He leans the framed portrait against a cold gravestone. Slowly lets go his hands as a parent leaves a child on the first day of school.

Eyes looking forward, but only seeing the past, unfocused, sweating. The incense finally burns its way into them. The Major coughs, stumbles up to his feet. He remembers there are others buried here. And that he is still alive. Out of the corner of his eye, another person. The Major's lonely heart speaks, "Arlen was a good young man."

Jinshirou quietly nods.

The Major takes his eyes off Arlen's photo for the first time, narrows his eyelids at all the teeth. "So many dead young men. You have to... have to... uhm, I'm... I'm not sure it was really..."

His upward peer momentary only, the Major's head drops back down in sadness. He catches a glimpse of Jin's bare feet. For the first time in several days, the Major begins to see beyond his own misery, beyond the photo, scans up along Jin's big Japanese body. His voice strengthens. "Arlen. He was my grandson." The Major clears his throat as to be crystal clear with the following question, "How did *you* know him?"

Jinshirou, eyes to stone to teeth, doesn't turn his head, doesn't look away. Response is soft, but distinctly audible, "I killed him."

Now like stones too, the Major's eyes crack, rush over with water, then close. He lowers his head very slowly, calmly, without emotion, right hand pops the holster strap, grips pistol. A deep breath, draws the weapon, turns it to Jin's head.

Jin drops to his knees, the grass breaks beneath. Cold dirt embraces him. His head folds slowly down, peacefully waiting to be shot. The icy barrel cools against his skull. Jin wishes the bullet out of its chamber. Calls it. Beckons it. "Come sweet bird" Jin sings inside, "snatch me from thse air."

Like the temple bells half the world away, the steel gun vibrates against Jin's ear. A finger trembles at the trigger, a bird readies at the perch.

"Blreak my fragile wings."

"You fuckin' jap!" The Major looks out over all the graves, all the dead American soldiers. A thrust of breath streams from his nostrils, "You god damned murderer!"

"Take my flight, swallow me whole, let my frlesh gib you life."

The Major grabs a chunk of Jin's hair, he shoves the gun harder into Jin's skull.

"Your grandmother, my grandson." The gun barrel breaks skin, touches bone. "What? Is it my turn again? My turn to kill somebody's grandson?"

Like a sharpened icicle sliding into his melting soul, the pistol scrapes against Jin's thick white skull. Jin's song fades, fear falls upon him with the weight of a screaming freight train, trembles like a child's top at final spin.

The Major pushes Jin's head to the ground, Jin's gashed forehead in front of Arlen's photo. Jin's tears flow, beneath the grass, roots suck them up. Something silver drops near his ear, then another. A battery, no, a bullet. Then another, then the gun. Jin, twitching like a stick of incense in the wind, rolls his head toward the gun. Grass, gun, bullets.

"By God, it's not gonna be me this time!" The Major kicks Jin in the shoulder. Jin falls sideways, curls like a fetus. The Major kicks him again. "I will not be the one continuing this... this..." The Major stumbles in thought, in so many bloody memories.

Jin can only see the gun, the grass, the fallen bullets, Arlen's photo. Then the Major's boot crushes the sticks of smoke, grinds them to dirt.

"This is my grandson!" The Major shouts, his words finding chords in his voice box seldom used before, "I don't go sobbin' over your grandma's ashes!" A snarl flashes, for a second, he feels an animal inside. But he kicks that animal, then kicks the frozen Jin's left kidney. "Get the hell out of here!"

Jin welcomes the pain, but feels none. The Major picks up the bagged burger and bounces it down against Jin's face. "I said -- *Get the hell out!*"

Jin comes face to face with life. His dreams of death dashed, thwarted with such harsh mercy that all honor escapes him, flies away like a pigeon. It would have been so much easier to die.

"Get the fuck up, and get the hell out!"

Jin, dizzy, body wobbles to vertical. Unsteady, his frame can hardly find balance.

"Stay away, you! Don't you come back here!"

Jin staggers away. His back toward the Major, at twenty paces he stops, turns suddenly, with the crying eyes of a little boy, "Thsank you."

"Get!"

The Major picks bullets from the ground, throws them one by one until the retreating Jin can no longer be seen past the domino chain of concrete tombstones.

.

Mrs. Williams walks through the museum. On the wall, a young boy's burnt skin hangs from his arm like a shirt, a man's eyes dangle from their sockets, a woman charred like fish. Mrs. Williams brings her hands to her face, her red, soft, suede gloves comfort her pale skin, absorb a tear. The images are too much to bear so she turns from them to a diary encased in glass.

THE END

ORDERING & FEEDBACK INFORMATION

☎PHONE
800-ROSS-186 (1-800-767-7186)
Book Ross to speak at your organization or school.
Q&A, Writing & Revision, World Travel, Film Reviewing, etc.
Remind him to bring his handmade flute.
RossAnthony.com/books/guestspeaker.shtml
RossAnthony.com/books/showtix.shtml

✉MAIL
Jinshirou...$10   Eddie...$10   Rodney...$10   Snail...$10   Ants...$10

Cal Tax included in price - Shipping/Handling...$5
Pay to the Order of Ross Anthony * Include your ship-to address
These prices good through 2005 after that -- inquire by phone.

Ross Anthony
P.O. Box 5
Pasadena, CA 91102

🖳ONLINE
www.RossAnthony.com/books
Check out other Ross Anthony books there.
And read some of his free essays & articles too.
Books sometimes become movies and movies get reviewed at...
www.HollywoodReportCard.com
Film Reviews and Interviews by Ross Anthony
Ross@RossAnthony.com (Subject: ARK!)

Also by Ross Anthony

Books

Eddie Johnson's Ark

A lumberyard tale for those of us under construction.
Eddie's a single parent raising three kids in Columbus, Ohio. He's working nine to five just to keep a roof over their heads when he receives an unexpected and supernatural visit in his kitchen. A very dead friend rummaging through his refrigerator for beer, delivers a message from God,
"It's time for a flood Eddie, stop whatever you're doing and build an Ark."
For mature audiences, some strong language.

The Infinite Adventures of Rodney Appleseed
In Nothing Happens

Rodney is curious, a thinker, an asker of questions and a wonderer. Join him in his daydreams as they twist, turn, and tangent. You won't know what's real, he won't know what's real, but you'll both revel in good fun and thought within this surreal adventure. Strengthened with philosophy, accented with culture, and frosted with a positive message -- this book is truly unique. Clean, though likely too conceptual for readers under age eight -- teens and adults love it!

The Little Snail Story

Like Saint-Exupery's "Little Prince," disguised as a children's book, "Little Snail" is a timeless story of gathering understanding, trust and belief in oneself. A friendly, insightful encouraging story for anyone hesitant to live an enriching vivacious life.

Short Essays

Zen of Surfing
A River Runs Through You
Graduation Boy
In the Dark (A 911 Tribute)

Celebrity Interviews

Harrison Ford
Meg Ryan
Michelle Pfeiffer
Johnny Knoxville
Antonio Banderas, etc.